THE MEMORY OF ALL THAT

NANCY SMITH GIBSON

Enjoy!

Nancy Smith Gibson

SOUL MATE PUBLISHING

New York

THE MEMORY OF ALL THAT

Copyright©2015

NANCY SMITH GIBSON

Cover Design by Leah Kaye-Suttle

Published in the United States of America by
Soul Mate Publishing
P.O. Box 24
Macedon, New York, 14502

ISBN: 978-1-68291-075-7

ebook ISBN: 978-1-61935-818-8

www.SoulMatePublishing.com

The Memory Of All That *is dedicated to my family,*

who have always encouraged me to follow my dreams.

Thank you Lisa Gibson Sanderock,

Robin Gibson Beard, Holly Gibson Thorwarth,

and James Joel Gibson for your love and support.

Acknowledgements

My deepest thanks to all those who helped me get this book written and published. My special thanks to the Hot Springs Critique and Feedback Group, who listened and made suggestions to improve the story. Special thanks are due to my diligent editor, Tamus Bairen, without whom this novel would be full of mistakes.

Chapter 1

The first thing she saw when she opened her eyes was the man sitting in a chair beside the bed. His expression was solemn, and his dark blue eyes were fixed on her. When he saw she was awake, he frowned but said nothing. She began to open her mouth to ask where she was, but the blackness closed in again.

She didn't know how long she had slept, but the next time she opened her eyes, the chair by the bed was empty. Smelling the faint scent of aftershave, she scanned the room and saw the man standing in the doorway with his hand on the doorknob, looking back at her.

Handsome, she thought, *but he looks so sad.*

Before she could gather her thoughts and strength enough to speak, he left, closing the door behind him.

Now that she was able to stay awake long enough to survey her surroundings, she observed deep red, flocked wallpaper and rosewood crown molding against the high ceiling. Maroon tapestry draperies covered the windows, shutting out any potential sunlight. The lamp on the bedside table offered scant illumination for the large room. The white sheets and duvet covering the four-poster bed were the only relief from the dreariness the dark colors instilled. *This room is straight out of a Gothic novel*, she thought.

She sighed and closed her eyes, unable to keep them open any longer. Before the black claimed her again, she tried to make sense of what had happened and how she had ended up in this room.

The icy-cold mist on her cheeks—that was the first thing she remembered. It stung as if someone had slapped her.

Looking around, she saw she was standing in a small grove of trees. The pine needles under her feet released a pungent odor. About twenty feet away, there was a picnic table, a grill, and playground equipment. She took a few steps, slipping slightly on the pine needles mixed with sodden leaves. She grabbed hold of a low hanging, bare branch to steady herself. That's when she noticed the street running beside the park. She turned toward it when a thought hit her. The power of it caused her legs to grow weak, and she almost fell to the ground.

She had no idea where she was or what she was doing there. *What's going on? How could I not know where I am?* Her mind tried to make sense of the situation. *Maybe I've had an accident and I'm in shock.* She tried to recall anything that happened before she felt the moisture on her face, but nothing came to her. The past before that moment was a blank.

Then another thought struck her so violently that she wrapped her arms around a small tree in order to remain standing. *Not only do I not know where I am, I don't know who I am. I don't even know my name.* She tightened her hold on the support. *What can I do? I can't just stand here in the cold rain. Where can I go?*

Panic washed over her like an ocean wave, threatening to pull her under. She had nothing to hold to, no memories, no facts, nothing beyond what was in the here and now, but she had no idea where "here and now" was.

Across the street, a woman with her arms full of packages met a policeman walking the opposite direction. They stopped and chatted, and she thought, *Maybe I should go say something to that policeman. Tell him I'm lost. Tell him I don't know who I am. Ask for his help. But what could he do? Take me to a hospital? Take me to jail? Put my picture in the newspaper and ask if anyone knows me? Any of that would be so embarrassing. And my memory will come back any second now . . . any second.*

Before she could act, the pair separated and went different ways.

Just as well, she thought as she started toward where they had stood. *I would probably end up in a psychiatric ward somewhere. And I'm not crazy. I know I'm not. I just can't remember who I am.*

When she reached the sidewalk, an idea occurred to her, and she stopped to study the clothing she was wearing. Brown leather boots extended to just below her knees, and she was enfolded in a brown wool coat with a muted orange plaid pattern. It was fastened with large brown buttons and held closed with a belt of the same fabric.

Why am I wearing this awful coat? As quickly as that notion had come to her came another. *How do I know I don't like a brown and orange coat? It is ridiculous to know what clothes I don't like and not know anything else.*

There was a purse strap on her arm. *Now I'll find some answers. There's sure to be a driver's license or credit card or something else with my name and address on it in this handbag.* All she found in the bag was some loose change, a tissue, and a small mirror.

At least I can see what I look like, she thought. Raising the mirror to her face, she saw a young woman—perhaps in her late twenties. She was attractive, with coffee-colored eyes. Dark brown hair curled out from beneath the ugliest scarf she had ever seen.

What is it with these clothes? she thought. *How come I'm wearing stuff I don't like?*

She put the mirror back in the purse and snapped the old-fashioned clasp. Continuing along the sidewalk, she passed several shops and then paused in front of a café.

If I had enough money I could go inside and get a cup of coffee.

She only found forty-one cents in the purse, not enough for coffee, and she couldn't imagine going in the café and asking if anyone in there knew who she was. She stuck her hands in the coat pockets and felt the rustle of paper. Eagerly, she pulled it from her pocket and smoothed it between her fingers. "Nicole's Fashions" was written across the top. It was a receipt for a dress shop. It also read, "Two dresses. $178. Deliver to 1532 Springhill Drive."

Finally! This must be where I live. 1532 Springhill Drive. How do I find it?

Another puzzle. She walked aimlessly past another couple of stores and glanced at the sign marking an intersection. *Springhill Drive.*

OK. So I'll walk home. When I get to that address, it will be home, and I'll remember it.

She crossed the thoroughfare and started walking up Springhill Drive.

Maybe I've had the flu. Yes, I think that's it. I've had the flu and I've been really, really sick. I remember that! That's what's happened. That's why I don't remember anything else. When I see my house, it'll all come back.

She walked for blocks. It was late afternoon, and though it was cloudy and overcast, she could tell it was growing later. Lights were on in the modest houses she walked by. As she passed, a car pulled into the driveway of a neat, white frame home. A man got out, and children rushed from the house, calling "Daddy! Daddy!"

Tears welled in her eyes. *Do I have a husband somewhere worrying about me? Wondering what has become of me? Do I have children needing their mother? Have I been gone long? Has anyone called the police to report me missing?* The questions filled her mind and smothered her in despair. *Surely someone is looking for me.*

By the time she walked a few blocks, the mist had turned to snow, and she began to feel feverish and weak. By the ten hundred block, she was beginning to doubt she could make it another five, but the alternative was embarrassing—unthinkable. Either she could go until she fell down or she could walk up to a strange door and ask for help. Neither option was acceptable to her. She would just have to push on until she found 1532. The farther she went, the larger and more affluent the houses became, and she began to have doubts about the possibility of living in such an obviously wealthy neighborhood. It didn't feel right, and nothing looked the least bit familiar. She believed it more likely she lived in one of the modest homes than the current mansions she was seeing. *Maybe I work at one of these big houses. Maybe I'm a maid or a personal assistant or something.*

By the time she determined she could walk no more, snow was rapidly covering the ground. She was alternating between hot and freezing, with a black cloud moving in on the sides of her vision. She stopped and leaned up against a tall column marking the opening in a red brick wall where a driveway led to an imposing house built of the same material.

I can't go any more. As embarrassed as I might be, I have to ask for help. Maybe someone is at home here. If I can make it to the front door, I'll have to make them understand.

Her hand touched a brass plate on the pillar, and she turned her head to read it. 1532 Springhill Road. She had found what she was looking for.

I can make it that far. If it's not my house, whoever lives here will just have to help me. I can't do anything else. She was about ten feet from the wide stone steps leading up to the massive front door when it opened and a tiny woman dressed in a black uniform and white apron rushed out.

"Miss Marnie! Miss Marnie! I knew you'd come back! She said you wouldn't, but I knew you would."

Marnie. My name is Marnie. She was glad she knew her name, but it didn't bring back any recollection of her past. *I must be home. This woman knows me.*

As the diminutive woman put her arm around Marnie and helped her up the steps and through the door, the blackness crept in, but she held on to consciousness for all she was worth.

"That's it. One more step, Miss Marnie. And another. You can make it. We'll get you to bed. You just lean on me, and I'll get you to your room. One more step. That's it."

When they were about halfway up the flight of steps leading to the second floor, a voice came from the downstairs hall. They paused, and Marnie looked over the rail at the gray-haired woman below.

"So you're back, are you? Well, let me tell you something. This time you've gone too far. This time you'll end up in prison. I'll see to it."

Chapter 2

Each time Marnie awoke, she saw the woman in the maid's uniform asleep in a chair. If Marnie moved, the woman woke up and hurried to her side. If Marnie was burning with fever, she wiped her face and hands with a cool, wet cloth. When Marnie was shivering with a chill, she fetched a hot water bottle to tuck at her feet.

Once, when Marnie was free of fever and chills, the woman helped her out of bed and down a short hall to a large white-tiled bathroom. A big, claw-foot tub sat under a high window, and a walk-in shower filled the opposite wall. Marnie changed out of her sweat-soaked pajamas with the woman's assistance and into a clean pair. Marnie vaguely remembered the woman helping her undress and slip into soft cotton pants and a top with tiny pink roses on them when she first arrived. Now she put on a mint green pair, warm and comforting.

"You can wear some of your fancy silk nightgowns when you're feeling better. These will be more comfortable until your fever breaks for good," the old woman said.

I have silk nightgowns? The thought seemed incongruous, somehow. Even now, with no memory of her past, she couldn't even imagine herself in such a garment.

Gradually the time she was free of both fever and chills lengthened, and although she was terribly weak, she rested more comfortably. When she awoke again, she saw daylight shining around the edges of the heavy drapes.

The night is over, and I have lived through it! It surprised her to realize she had had doubts about it.

Voices in the hall alerted her to visitors before they entered the room. First through the door was the tall, handsome man who had been sitting in the chair beside the bed. His dark hair was brushed smooth, and he was dressed in a business suit and tie. His expression was still solemn, even grim. Behind him was an older man, short and balding. The black bag he carried identified him as a doctor. The maid who had helped Marnie followed the men into the bedroom, chattering away.

"She woke up throughout the night. One time she'd be burning up with the fever. Next she'd be shivering with chills. About dawn, her temperature seemed to break."

"You're doing a fine job of caring for her, Alice," the doctor said.

"Are you sure she shouldn't be in the hospital, Doctor Means?" the handsome man asked. His voice was low and smooth. Marnie wasn't sure if the tingle that ran through her was from his voice or the chills.

"Of course she should be, but as I explained last night, every bed in the local hospital is full. We'll keep a close eye on her, and if it seems like pneumonia is setting in, we'll have an ambulance take her to Memorial Hospital in Centerview. I'd like to avoid that trip if I can. It would be hard on her."

The doctor sat in the chair beside the bed and took out his stethoscope.

"So you're awake, young lady. Let me listen to your lungs."

When he finished his examination, he removed the stethoscope.

"Well, your lungs are clear. Alice tells me you were able to get up and go to the bathroom during the night, and you drank some water. Is that right?"

She tried to answer, but her voice squeaked with the effort.

"You were pretty much out of it when I saw you last night. Do you remember when I was here?"

She tried to remember what happened after she arrived and was put to bed, but it was no use. She had been too incoherent then to recall any details now.

"No."

"Can you tell us where you've been? What's happened to you?"

She shook her head slightly. "I don't remember."

The doctor sighed and put the stethoscope back in its case.

"You're still very sick. Maybe you'll remember when you're better." He stood and turned to the handsome man.

"I'll come by again this afternoon after office hours, David." He turned toward Alice. "I'll call the pharmacy and have them send over some pills. Now that she's alert enough to swallow a capsule, I won't need to treat her by injection. See that she gets one every four hours. She's still very sick and needs the medicine on schedule."

The doctor picked up his bag and started toward the door, stopping in front of Alice. "If her temperature stays down, see if you can get her to eat a little broth. She needs some nourishment. And keep giving her water. If she can't drink water, we'll have to get her into the hospital or else set up something here. I don't want her becoming dehydrated."

"Marnie, I'll see you again this afternoon," he said as he walked out the door.

She heard his voice receding as he walked down the hall. "David, I don't want you questioning her. . . ." She was left wondering who David was to her and why he would want to question her. She hadn't experienced any chills or fever for several hours, but she still felt very weak. She closed her eyes and tried to sort out all she had been presented with since she made her way to this house.

The woman who came out the front door and helped her upstairs to her room was Alice. She seemed to like Marnie. She was gentle and caring toward her, sitting up with her all night and seeing to her needs. She soothed and petted like Marnie was her child. *But that can't be right, can it? No. No, it couldn't. Alice calls me Miss Marnie. She wouldn't call her own daughter "Miss."*

Doctor Means was straightforward enough. She thought it was unusual for a doctor to make house calls. He said the hospital was full, and she certainly was too weak to go to a doctor's office, so maybe that's why he came. She wondered if anyone else in the house would have taken care of her if it were necessary.

How am I connected to this man . . . David? His face is so serious each time I see him. Is it because he is worried about me? Has he been concerned about what happened to me? When he stood at the door that first time he looked angry and sad at the same time. Maybe he is my employer. Did I make some terrible mistake? Mess up something? That would explain why the woman I saw yesterday was so angry. But what kind of job do I have that entitles me to my own room here in this house?

Marnie couldn't image doing anything illegal, but the woman in the downstairs hall made it seem like she did. *Why else would she threaten to send me to jail?*

Oh, I don't know who I am, she thought. *I might do illegal things. I might be a terrible person. I just don't remember.* Marnie covered her face with her hands and shook her head. *How horrible that would be, to get my memory back and find out I'm a bad person!*

Her surroundings seemed strange to her, even though she obviously lived in the house. Her pajamas and gowns were here, because Alice had ready access to them. But it just didn't feel like a home should; it wasn't comfortable. Even with her memory gone, she instinctively knew she would want to live in a place with light, bright colors, and windows that let the sunlight in, not in this room of deep, dark shadows and oversized, intricately carved furniture. The sound of a bump against the door caused her to turn, and she saw a small figure dart out of sight.

Strange, she thought, *that looked like a child.* She yawned, closed her eyes, and drifted off to sleep.

Chapter 3

"Good afternoon, Marnie."

The doctor set his black leather bag on the table beside the bed and opened it. "Alice tells me your fever is down and you haven't had any more chills."

Marnie pulled herself a little higher in the bed. "That's right. I've had some fever, but nothing like before, and no chills."

Taking the thermometer out of his bag, he said, "Hold this under your tongue while I listen to your lungs. How have you felt today? Are you keeping the broth down all right? Drinking plenty of water?" He removed the thermometer from her mouth and checked the reading.

"I'm still very weak. Alice has to help me to the bathroom, and I slept most of the day. But I'm beginning to feel a little hungry."

"That's a good sign. I'll tell Alice to start giving you some soft food."

When he had finished his exam, he settled into the chair at her bedside. Folding his hands over his round belly, he surveyed her with a serious expression.

"Marnie, I've known you since you were just a little thing. I think you were about six years old when your mother first brought you in to see me. Do you remember that?"

She shook her head.

"You were getting your immunizations before starting first grade. From then on, you were in my office every few months to get patched up from one scrape or another. It seemed like you were always going somewhere you shouldn't or doing something dangerous.

"I remember when you followed some boys in the neighborhood when you were ten. They told you not to climb the ladder into their treehouse, so you climbed another tree and tried to jump over. You sure fussed at me about the cast on your broken arm. You would always do exactly what someone told you not to do. Remember what you once told me?"

As the doctor recounted her childhood, Marnie tried her best to remember it, but nothing came to her. Slowly, she shook her head.

"I don't remember, Doctor. I don't remember a thing. Not you, not this house, not even who I am."

He studied her intently. "Marnie, is this another one of your tricks?"

"No. It's not a trick. I can't remember anything."

He sat quietly for a few moments before speaking. "What is the first thing you do remember, and how did you come to be back home?"

"The first thing I remember is standing in a park right beside a city street, the cold mist stinging my cheeks."

She went on to tell him about finding the receipt and following the street to the address written on it, about being too weak to go on, and about Alice leading her to this room.

"I didn't know her name then, but she knew me. She called me 'Miss Marnie,' and that's how I found out my name. I don't know anything else about myself, though. Can you tell me, Doctor? Can you tell me who I am and why these people seem to be mad at me?"

The portly man simply stared at her. He appeared to be waiting for her to add more information to what she had already told him. Finally he spoke.

"I've seen many cases of temporary amnesia. People who have had a shock sometimes forget things. A person who's been in a mishap of some sort—a car wreck or industrial accident—may never remember it happening. And sometimes when something really terrible, emotionally speaking, has happened, people shut it out like it never happened because they can't deal with it. But I've never had anyone forget who they are or what has happened in their lives up until the time of the event. That's rare . . . very rare."

He continued to observe her, without a word. Finally he sighed and continued.

"I don't know if this is one of your tricks or not, Marnie"— he stood and picked up his satchel—"but I will tell you this: both David and Ruth are extremely upset with you. I don't know what you did for them to react like this, but it must be something serious. I'm glad I don't know. That keeps me from getting in the middle of something that's not my business. Besides, you need to remember things on your own, instead of claiming someone else's words as your memories. It would be too easy to tell you what you did or said and make you think that was the truth when it might not be so.

"I'm not saying anyone in your life would deliberately do that, but I've seen it happen in cases of severe trauma. You need to be the one to figure it out because you're the only person who knows what you did and why. You're the only person who can answer your questions."

"I wish I could remember, Doctor. Truly I do. It is a terrible feeling to not remember my past or even who I am."

"I would like to promise you your memory will come back, but I can't. It usually does, though." He turned and walked toward the door. "Just keep getting better. Take your medicine and rest. I'll tell Alice to give you some light food. Maybe in a couple of days you can get up. Maybe something in the house will jog your memory."

He paused before walking out of the room.

"Doctor, what did I say to you when I was ten?"

"You said, 'If I can't get to where I'm going one way, I'll get to it another.' You've pretty much lived by that rule all your life."

Chapter 4

Marnie sank back into the soft bedding, pulled the duvet around her shoulders to protect her from the chill in the room, and thought about what Doctor Means had said. She might eventually remember her life and what had happened to her, but there was a chance she might not. She didn't know if she could face the possibility of never knowing her past. She didn't know if she could build a life with the people around her being angry about something she couldn't remember doing. She wondered if she'd be able to make amends, especially if she didn't remember doing anything.

As she puzzled over seemingly insurmountable obstacles, she noticed the small face once again looking into the room from around door.

"Hi," she said, and the face disappeared.

She stayed quiet and still, and the face soon reappeared. He looked to be about five years old, and he had dark brown hair with bangs cut straight across. Chocolate eyes watched her curiously.

"Hi," she said again, expecting him to retreat as before.

He was silent as his eyes scanned the room and came to rest on Marnie.

"Hi," he said finally.

"What's your name?"

He appeared to be thinking about his answer, as if he, like Marnie, wasn't too sure.

"Jonathan."

"I'm pleased to meet you, Jonathan. I'm Marnie. But I guess you already knew that."

He didn't reply but turned his head and then darted away.

A minute later, Alice entered the room carrying a tray loaded with food.

"Doctor Means said you were getting hungry and could have some soft food, so I had Cook fix you some scrambled eggs and toast."

She set the tray on the bedside table and propped Marnie up on two fluffy pillows. The tray she placed across Marnie's legs was carefully set with fine china and real silver.

"This looks lovely, Alice."

"When you're feeling poorly, it helps to have a touch of pretty to make you feel better," Alice said as she took the napkin from the tray and spread it over Marnie's pajamas. When she removed the silver dome covering the plate, the aroma caused Marnie's stomach to growl in anticipation.

"Mm. This is delicious," she said after the first forkful.

"Yes, Cook knows just how you like 'em."

Then she knows more than I do, Marnie thought.

Alice sat in the chair next to the bed.

"You're doing a lot better. If you don't think you'll need me during the night, I'd like to go home and sleep in my own bed."

Marnie stopped, fork mid-air, and stared at her.

"If you think you'll need me, I'll stay," the older woman said as she hopped to her feet and smoothed the sheet covering Marnie.

"Alice, no. It's just that I never thought about where you were sleeping."

"I've been catching a few minutes shut-eye here and there in the rooms up on the top floor that the live-in help used in the old days. I can stay tonight," she said determinedly. "You might need me."

"No, Alice. You go on home. I've gotten up a couple of times by myself today, and I made it just fine. You go on home for the night."

"Well, if you're sure."

"I'm sure."

As Marnie finished the last few bites, Alice spoke again.

"Dr. Means said you can't remember what happened to you, where you've been and all."

Marnie leaned back and settled into the pillows.

"No, I can't. In fact, I can't remember anything at all."

"Isn't that something? Wonder why?"

"I don't know. The doctor said I'll probably remember in time, but it's possible I might never regain my memory."

"He's having dinner downstairs with Mr. David and Miss Ruth. They're all talking about what happened."

"What are they saying?"

Alice looked evasively around the room and twisted the hem of her apron. "I didn't stay. I don't listen in on conversations in the house."

"I didn't mean that, Alice. I just thought you might have heard him say more than he told me about what might have caused my amnesia."

"Well," she said as she smoothed her apron flat again, "he said it was most likely a shock of some kind, but that you looked right run down—that's what he said, 'run down'— and was really sick, not pretending."

"Not pretending to be sick or not pretending to have amnesia?"

"Not pretending to be sick. You're really sick."

"But I'm pretending to have amnesia?"

Alice shrugged her shoulders. "That's what they're talking about."

"I'm not pretending. I didn't even know my name until you called me Marnie."

"Land sakes," Alice said, her eyes growing wide. "Isn't that something?" She leaned forward in the chair. "You didn't even know your name?"

"No, not even that."

"How did you get here, home that is, if you didn't know who you was?"

"I found a receipt in my coat pocket that had this address on it, so I walked."

"Where did you walk from? Was it far?"

"The first thing I can remember is I was standing in a park. I started walking, passing stores and a café. I kept thinking I would remember at any minute who I was and where I belonged, but nothing came to me. When I found the receipt and saw the street sign, I just started walking until I got here."

"That was a long walk from City Park to here."

"Yes, and I couldn't have gone any further. If you hadn't come out of the house when you did, I probably would have passed out before I made it up the front steps."

Marnie was so intent on telling Alice her story she didn't hear the footsteps in the hall and was startled by the deep, masculine voice.

"Alice, would you leave us, please?"

"Yes, sir." She rose from the chair and picked up the tray that bridged Marnie's lap. "I'll just take this back to the kitchen now." She stopped in the doorway and turned around. "I'll check back on you, Miss Marnie, and get you settled for the night before I go home." She left, casting a glance at the stern-faced man who now stood by the bed.

"So, you don't remember anything before you appeared at the front door. Is that right?"

Marnie drew the soft white duvet around her neck, as if to protect herself from the question laden with sarcasm.

"Yes."

He sat down in the chair beside the bed.

"That's a dilly of a story, Marnie, even for you. Every time I think I couldn't be surprised by another thing you do or story you tell, you come up with something to top the last escapade." He crossed his legs and frowned. "Do you honestly think this is going to get you out of trouble?"

"I *don't* remember what I did. The first thing I remember is standing in the park, but from the way that woman spoke to me, threatening me with jail, and now your tone of voice, I must have done something horrible."

He snickered humorlessly. "You might say that."

"Well, whatever it was, I'm sorry."

"Sorry won't get it this time, Marnie."

"I might not remember my past, but I know myself, somehow. And I know I would never do anything horrible. I just wouldn't."

"So, you're remaking yourself? Just like that? You don't remember, so now you're a good girl?"

Marnie was trembling from the effort to be civil to this odious man. *How dare he tell me I'm not a good person?*

"I am. I *know* it."

"Well, you sure could have fooled me and everyone around you."

"Alice seems to like me. She speaks kindly to me."

"She's known you since you were a little girl. Perhaps she has better memories of you than the rest of us do."

He shoved the chair back and strode toward the door.

"Doctor Means said it's better if you remember on your own who you are and what you've done. So, I'm not going to give you any clues to your past. You'll slip up soon, and the game will be over."

He paused at the door to give her one final look, and she took the opportunity to ask him the question that had been plaguing her since she first saw him.

"Please tell me one thing. Are you David?"

He stared, unspeaking, and then nodded.

"Who are you to me? Are you my employer?"

His smile was bitter as he answered, "Surely you haven't forgotten that, my dear, after you tried so hard to catch me. I'm your husband."

Chapter 5

Marnie was stunned. So many questions swirled around in her brain she hardly knew which one to concentrate on first. David was her husband. Somehow that wasn't a complete shock. She remembered the tingle she felt when she first heard his voice. Her body evidently hadn't forgotten him, even if her brain had. Something deep within her woke up and paid attention when he spoke.

Were we ever in love? I can't imagine being married to someone I don't love and who doesn't love me in return. But then, I don't remember being married to anyone, much less this David person. Did his voice once whisper into my ear as we made love? Was that deep tone once kind and gentle, laughing and teasing instead of disbelieving and harsh?

It wasn't a memory, exactly, that was tugging at her mind. It was more like an awareness that David held some sort of an emotional pull over her. It wasn't much, but it was something to build on as she tried to retrieve her missing memories. She hoped these feelings meant her memory was coming back. She needed to learn why her husband was so angry with her.

She closed her eyes and recalled his face. Square and handsome, with blue eyes and dark brown hair, he had seemed worried, angry, or bitterly sarcastic each time she saw him. *Surely that isn't how he's always looked. He must have looked at me lovingly once, before all this trouble—whatever it is—started.* She tried to imagine him smiling at her, kissing her. She smiled herself as the image of his lips on hers flitted through her mind. *Is that a memory or my imagination? I can't tell.*

Marnie sighed and sat up, throwing the cover aside. She was sleepy again, although it seemed all she did was sleep. Sliding her legs over the edge, she gingerly stood up and made her way to the bathroom. She had rummaged through the cabinet that morning and found a new toothbrush and some toothpaste, and she used it to make her mouth fresh once again.

Not that he's going to kiss me, even if he is my husband, she thought. *He's too mad to do that. I'm not even sure I'd want him to. Since I don't remember him, it would be like kissing a stranger.* Suddenly, that thought was exciting, not scary.

Might as well get ready for bed. Taking a washcloth, she cleaned her face. Looking in the mirror, she surveyed the woman she saw. The shoulder-length hair that curled around a pale oval face was tousled and in need of a thorough washing.

Not beautiful, but it'll do. Maybe clean hair and some makeup would improve my appearance. Or maybe just getting well will.

She hung the cloth on the towel rack and started back toward the bed. With her strength gone, she held to the wall in the short hall back to the bedroom. Alice was there, straightening the bedcovers.

"I was just smoothing everything so you can rest. Maybe tomorrow, if you feel like it, you can shower and wash your hair, and I can change the sheets on the bed," Alice said as she gave the pillows a final punch.

"Yes. I was looking in the mirror and saw my hair. I hope I'll be up to doing that."

"There's a bench in the shower you can sit on while you wash, and I'll be here if you get to feeling shaky."

Marnie climbed into bed and fell asleep with thoughts of a hot shower and warm lips kissing hers.

As soon as Marnie stepped from the shower, Alice wrapped her in a terrycloth robe before she became chilled.

"Do you want to put pajamas back on or do you want to get dressed today?"

"Do I own any sweats? I don't really want to get dressed, but I don't want PJs either."

"Why don't you look in your closet, Miss Marnie? I don't know what all you have."

"Where is my closet?"

"Land sakes! You don't even remember where your closet is?" She walked into the hallway between the bedroom and bathroom. "It's right here," she said and opened a door Marnie had noticed earlier. "This is yours, and the one on the other side,"—she pointed across the hall—"is Mr. David's."

Racks of clothes filled two walls, while the outside wall held a window surrounded by drawers and shelves. A chair was handy for donning shoes, and a cheval mirror offered her a full-length view.

She was stunned by the abundance of clothing in every color and fabric. There were lace, satin, and silk evening gowns, some adorned with beads and sequins, each more elaborate and beautiful than the last. Suits of wool, silk, and other cloth took up several feet, followed by casual dresses in a variety of styles and colors. The rack on the other side held slacks and a whole section of jeans. There were blouses and shirts, along with skirts. Marnie couldn't imagine wearing a skirt as short as the ones hanging in her closet. In fact, she couldn't imagine where she would wear most of the clothes. *I must go to a lot of formal events to need all these evening clothes.* There were several coats, including the brown plaid one she had on when she woke up in the park.

She pulled out a long-sleeved shirt from among the casual clothing she thought might be comfortable to wear and found "Bitch" written in sparkling stones across the front. Shuddering, she hung it back on the rack. *Why on earth would I buy a shirt like that?*

She settled on a set of pink sweats. They weren't plain, but they didn't have vulgarities plastered across the front, and they would be warm and comfortable. She checked the drawers for underwear but found only scarves, belts, jewelry, and tank tops.

Alice came to the open closet door and peered in.

"Are you doing OK?"

"Yes, but I can't find any panties."

"You keep those in a drawer in the bedroom. You ran out of room in here."

"I can't imagine why I would need all these clothes."

"Well, you might not need them, but you like them. You like to shop."

"I do?"

"You sure do. You and Mr. David—" She stopped midsentence and turned back toward the bedroom. "Let me get you some underwear."

When Alice returned, Marnie asked, "Mr. David and I what? What were you going to say?"

"Nothing. I'm not going to talk about what goes on between you two. And I'm not supposed to tell you anything about your past." She closed her mouth tightly, as if to prevent any more words from spilling out.

"Is that what he's mad at me about? Buying too many clothes? Spending too much money?"

"It's none of my business. I'm not saying another thing."

Marnie put on the warm outfit and rummaged through the drawers until she found some socks for her cold feet. Even though she sat in the chair while she dressed, she was exhausted by the time she was through and returned to the bedroom.

"Here, let me help you back into the bed. You've done enough for now."

"Let me just lie on top of the covers, Alice. I'll rest a while, and maybe I'll feel like getting up again."

When Alice spread a cover over her, Marnie roused slightly from her sleep and then sank back into slumber.

When she awoke again, it was to Alice bringing a lunch tray.

"That smells delicious! I'm getting hungry more often. When can I have solid food?"

"The doctor didn't say, but I'll see what I can do about getting a more substantial supper tonight. You're doing fine on soft food for now. This potato soup is good, and I brought pudding for dessert."

After Marnie had eaten, she set the tray aside and walked over to the large window that overlooked the yard. She was determined not to spend all of her time sleeping. She was surprised to see that a thick blanket of snow covered the landscape. She sat in one of the wingback chairs that were on either side of the window, separated by an accent table and lamp. As she looked around the room, she tried to remember having sat in the chair before, with no luck. The heavy drapes had been pulled back, allowing sunlight to brighten her mood slightly.

This could be a pleasant room, she thought, *if it were decorated with lighter colors.* She couldn't help but feel a little depressed and somewhat claustrophobic with the red patterned wallpaper, maroon drapes, and dark rug on the wood floor.

Maybe light blue or pale green on the walls would help cheer the place up. And light-colored drapes to match and a rug with spring flowers or some other happy pattern. That's what it needs. I can't believe I liked this room before.

Besides the bed, there were two large pieces of furniture in the room: a highboy and a dresser. Decorated ornately with carved flowers and leaves, their appearance added to the heaviness of the décor. *Those furniture pieces would fit just fine in a room with a lighter color scheme,* she thought.

She walked across the room and opened a dresser drawer. It contained a mish-mash of items, from makeup to jewelry, pieces of paper, cards, and a jumble of unidentifiable items. The next drawer and the one after held underwear. All of the rest of the drawers were filled with clothing of one sort or another.

She went to the highboy standing by the hallway door that led to the bathroom. The drawers were almost empty, and the few items she found obviously belonged to a man.

David's, she thought.

She felt like she had been snooping, prying into someone else's life. *Silly,* she thought. *I'm snooping in my own life. I wish something would spark a memory.*

Windows flanked the four-poster bed, and she went to examine the view they afforded. There she saw a circular drive, the one she staggered up when Alice had rescued her. Inside the red brick wall that bordered the street were bushes, now laden with snow.

At the end of her strength, she was shaking with fatigue. Climbing back in the bed, she propped herself up against the pile of snowy white pillows. *I don't feel the least bit sleepy,* she thought. *That's an improvement.*

As she continued to mentally redecorate the room, Jonathan appeared in the doorway with an oversized but thin book under his arm.

"Hi."

This time he didn't have to think before answering. "Hi."

"What do you have there?"

"A book."

"I can see that. What's it about?"

"Dinosaurs."

"Cool! Would you like to show me?"

He nodded and approached the bed.

"Climb on up here so I can see it."

In seconds Jonathan stretched out beside her so he could see the pictures while she read about the mighty beasts. He pointed out his favorites and told her bits of information about each.

They were admiring a particularly nice Tyrannosaurus when a woman appeared in the doorway. She was pretty, with a mass of blond hair surrounding her face. She was perfectly made-up and dressed in light blue slacks and matching cardigan. The top several buttons had been left undone, creating a stunning show of cleavage where a strand of pearls rested. *An outfit to catch a man,* Marnie thought.

"There you are! Darling, come along." She held her hand out toward the boy. "I'm so sorry, Mrs. Barrett. He slipped away from me. I hope he didn't disturb you."

"Not at all. I enjoyed his company."

"Sweetheart," the woman said in a syrupy voice, "you know you are supposed to play in your room." With that she turned to walk away, but Jonathan gave a little wave and a grin before following.

So my last name is Barrett, Marnie thought. *That woman must be Jonathan's mother. I wonder how they are connected with this family, why they live in this house. Are they relatives, perhaps?*

Alice arrived carrying the usual tray.

"My goodness, Alice. It's not suppertime already, is it? Although, I'll admit I could eat something right now."

Alice chuckled. "No, it's not suppertime for another couple of hours. Doctor Means called to see how you're doing, and he said to start feeding you more. He thinks you are real run-down and too thin. 'She needs fattenin' up' is what he said. Cook baked cookies, and I've brought you some and a glass of milk."

"Put them over there on the table, Alice. I'm going to try to get out of bed more."

"Doc said your strength would start to come back as you get over whatever is wrong with you. He said you looked like you hadn't been eating right—that's why you're so thin."

"I'll bet Jonathan likes these cookies," she said as she took a bite of the sugary treat.

"He surely does. He's on his way to get some now."

"The woman who came for him is lovely—so pretty." Marnie looked expectantly at Alice, hoping to gain some information about the other residents of the house.

"Well, she thinks she is, anyway," Alice said with a snort as she left the room.

Chapter 6

The next few days passed slowly as Marnie gradually regained her strength. She spent more and more time out of bed, first sitting in one of the chairs in her bedroom, and then venturing into the hall to sit in the window seat at the closest end of the passageway where she could look out over the side yard.

Jonathan was her companion most days. He would bring a book, usually the one about dinosaurs, and they would sit together while she read to him. Marnie wondered how she was able to remember details about the giant creatures but not her own life.

"Have I read this book to you before? That is, before I got sick?"

He shook his head.

As he went to retrieve another book, she noticed he entered a room about halfway down the hall.

"Is that your room?"

"Yes. Would you like to see it?"

He realizes I can't remember the past. Finally, someone who doesn't think I'm lying.

"Yes, I would," she answered, and he took her by the hand.

The room they entered was a playroom. Against one wall, there was a large bookcase with perhaps half a dozen books on a shelf. There were several plastic tubs on the shelf below, and she walked over and pulled one out, then another, to see the contents. One was filled with blocks of all colors and shapes and another with cars and trucks. An adult-sized table and chairs sat between the windows, and a child's table with only one chair centered the room. She wondered if he ever had a friend come to play. If so, there wouldn't be a place for them both to sit unless they used the big table.

The room itself did nothing to proclaim it was a little boy's room. The beige wallpaper was past its prime. Dark woodwork trimmed the walls at the ceiling and floor. An old patterned rug offered a less than pleasing place for a child to sit and play. It looked more like an adult's spot for reading, since a rocking chair that sat against one wall was flanked by a table holding a lamp. It was as if someone had put the children's table and shelves in as an afterthought. The sunlight pouring in the windows did nothing to alleviate the gloomy atmosphere. *It looks like no one cares about what he has to keep him happy,* she thought. *No one has given much thought to what a child needs. This is a forgotten place.*

Marnie wondered where the pretty blonde woman was. She hadn't seen her with Jonathan again.

"Where's your mother?" she asked.

He shrugged and examined the plastic dinosaur in his hands. "I don't know."

"Where do you sleep?" she asked.

"In here," he said, taking her hand once more to lead her through a door that connected to the next room.

At least in this room someone had taken the time to make the room more child friendly. The bed was an ordinary twin bed, but the spread on it resembled a racecar, and a bright blue fuzzy throw rug was placed on the floor beside it, tempting little toes to curl into its softness. The draperies at the tall windows were the color of a bright summer day, and there was a large stuffed bear on the bed.

"Oh, what a lovely bear. Does he have a name?"

Jonathan shrugged again. "Just Bear."

"Did someone special give it to you?"

"My mother," he said, still looking down at the toy in his hands. She could barely hear him as he answered.

"That makes it special, then, if your mother gave it to you."

He was silent at that pronouncement.

Jonathan and Marnie were together most days, walking the length of the hall as Marnie's strength returned. They would walk to Jonathan's playroom, where she would sit in the big overstuffed chair and read to him from one of the few choices available. Then they would walk to the far end of the hall and sit in the window seat, which was just like the one that was close to her room. They would rest a while before returning to her room. As the days wore on, Marnie felt stronger and no longer felt the need to nap as often.

A week or so later, Marnie was dressing for the day in a pair of jeans and a yellow cashmere sweater. As she stood in front of the mirror, she couldn't help but notice the changes in her appearance since she had arrived. Her color was better. Her cheeks were pink instead of the sickly white she had seen when she first ventured out of bed. Her face had filled out, and she no longer looked as gaunt. The clothes, which had been loose when she started wearing them instead of pajamas, fit nicely now. She felt better physically, if not mentally.

She decided the time had come to venture downstairs. Alice and Mary, another maid, took turns bringing Marnie's meals to her, but that was bound to be an extra duty for them. Marnie thought she was probably strong enough to manage the long flight of steps to the ground floor, and she knew it was time she started taking her meals in a more convenient location. She wondered if everyone in the household took their meals together.

Let's see. There's my husband, David. It's odd that he doesn't visit me more often, but that must have something to do with him being mad at me. I wish the doctor hadn't told everyone to withhold information from me so I would remember on my own. It isn't working. I'm not remembering anything. I wish I knew more about this odd family and how they are related to me and each other. Jonathan and his mother—how do they fit into the family? And who was the woman who said I was going to jail? It won't be very pleasant dining with people who are angry with me and no one telling me why, but if that's what it takes to remember my past, I'll do it.

Marnie thought about Jonathan's mother. She had seemed pleasant enough, but Marnie remembered thinking how odd her smile was. It looked like the fake smile you give someone you didn't really like. Or the smile someone gave when they knew a secret. *Maybe she's mad at me, too, for the unforgiveable sin I committed.*

Going downstairs for breakfast and exploring the main living quarters afterward seemed to Marnie like a great idea. *Maybe something will seem familiar. I can rest before going back up to my bedroom. Or if I don't wear myself out with that, perhaps I can stay downstairs for lunch.* Marnie wondered how she had spent her days before she lost her memory. Surely she had something to occupy her time. Evidently there were at least two maids, Alice and Mary, and a cook, so she doubted she did the housework. Maybe she had a job. A glimmer of memory flitted through her mind and then was gone. A job. *Yes, that is it. I worked, but what did I do?*

She hoped something downstairs would jog her memory. Nothing she had seen upstairs had done the trick. The only thing that seemed at all familiar was reading the children's books to Jonathan and the little plastic dinosaurs he constantly played with.

Suddenly, the door to the hall opened, and David stormed in, slamming it behind him.

"I never thought you would stoop so low as to use Jonathan in whatever game you're playing now!"

"What? What are you talking about?"

"You, you and this amnesia story you've got going on. You have everyone else stirred up. You have Alice waiting on you hand and foot, and now you've pulled Jonathan into it for your amusement."

"My memory loss is *not* a story. It's true. I'm sorry Alice has had to wait on me. Pardon me for not just lying down and dying. Maybe that would have been easier for you. I don't see how any of that has anything to do with my being friendly to Jonathan. It seems to me he could use a friend."

"Jonathan has people who care for him a hell of a lot more than you do. You've done nothing but use him for your own twisted purposes all his life. You've ignored him for four years. *Now* you decide to be his friend? I don't think so."

"Me? I used Jonathan for 'my own twisted purposes,' as you put it? How? How could I use a child that way?"

"By getting pregnant in the first place, my dear," he said in a sarcastic tone. "You used him to trap me into marriage and kept me in it."

"Jonathan? I—"

"Yes, Jonathan. Are you claiming you don't remember that Jonathan is your child?"

Using all of her strength, she clung to the bedpost, but it didn't hold her up when the blackness closed in and she sank to the floor.

Chapter 7

When she regained consciousness, she was lying on the bed and Doctor Means was speaking.

"Nothing seems to be physically wrong. She's not had a relapse. That is, she isn't running a fever, and her color is good. She's been on the mend this week, getting better all along. You say she fainted when you told her Jonathan is her child?"

The deep velvet voice that had so recently been disparaging answered. "Yes. She was acting like she didn't know it, and when I said he was hers, she turned white and fainted."

"It was the shock of learning that bit of information, I'm sure, that caused her to faint."

"Do you think her memory has returned? That is, if it really was missing?"

"David, I think you are going to have to accept the fact that her memory is, in fact, gone, at least temporarily. This shock, this fainting, may have brought it back, or maybe she fainted because it came back so suddenly. We'll just have to wait and see."

Marnie stirred on the bed and let out a low groan.

"She's waking up," Alice said from the other side of the bed.

"Marnie, do you remember what happened?" the doctor asked in a kind voice.

"Yes," she said. She covered her face with her hands. "David told me Jonathan is my son. I didn't remember. I didn't remember my own son." She burst into tears and rolled into a fetal position as her cries of distress echoed throughout the room. She wrapped her arms around herself as if trying to hold in the emotion, but her wailing grew worse. The doctor moved closed and helplessly patted her on the shoulder. Even David looked discomfited at his wife's obvious pain.

"Isn't there something you can do, Doctor?" Alice asked.

"A sedative maybe? Or a shot to calm her?" David questioned.

"No, I don't dare give her anything like that. The lab work came back on the blood I drew that first night. She was full of a narcotic of some sort. I don't know what exactly unless I send it off for more testing. Our little hospital lab couldn't tell my any more than that, but with her memory loss, I don't dare give her any more sedatives."

Gradually, Marnie's weeping grew quieter.

"Alice, get a warm washcloth for her, please," the doctor asked.

When Alice returned with the cloth, Marnie sat up and took it to wipe her face.

"Can you tell us why you were so upset to learn that Jonathan is your son? Do you remember your life with him?"

Her breathing was uneven, coming in sobs, and her body shuddered.

"No. I . . . it . . . it w-was something that washed o-over me in a wave. When David told me he was my son, the blackness closed in, just like it did when I was sick. When I came to, the sadness overwhelmed me."

"What about his being your son makes you sad? Are you unhappy about it?"

"Oh no! No! I'm not unhappy about him at all. I just didn't know . . . I didn't know he was my son. How could I have forgotten something like that—something so important? Maybe the news that I had ignored Jonathan for four years caused me to black out. How could I do that? My own son . . ." The tears started rolling down her cheeks again.

David had turned away and was pacing back and forth as she spoke.

"Now, now. Don't get worked up again." Doctor Means turned. "Alice, get her a glass of water."

"But that's so horrid! I'm a horrid person! How could I do that to my own son?"

David stopped at the foot of the bed and stared at her.

"Marnie, I find it hard to believe you're acting this time. If you are, then you're a better actress than you were before you left. Your lies usually drip with sweetness."

Alice returned from the bathroom with a glass of water, and Doctor Means encouraged Marnie to sip it slowly and regain her composure. "David, there is no way she was faking that much emotion."

She finally spoke again. "The sadness was suddenly overwhelming. It was as if I was mourning the loss of the last four years instead of my shortcomings as a mother."

"Have any of your memories returned this week?"

"Not really. But Jonathan had me read his dinosaur book several times, and it seemed familiar. I knew more facts about dinosaurs than were in the book, and I don't know where I learned them. I don't remember dinosaurs being especially interesting to me."

"I don't remember you ever reading that book—or any book—to him," David said. "I read it to him, as did Mrs. Tucker, but not you. You didn't play with him much."

Marnie bit her lip in an attempt to hold back the tears.

Uncharacteristically kind, David said, "I'm not saying that to blame you for anything, just to set the record straight. If you know about dinosaurs, it's not from reading that book to Jonathan, as far as I know. Maybe it's from your own childhood."

Doctor Means spoke again. "Anything else, Marnie? Anything you remember?"

"The little plastic toy dinosaurs he plays with. When I hold one, it seems very familiar."

David spoke again. "He is never without one, either in his hand or in his pocket. You're used to seeing him with one."

"So you are getting a bit of your memory back. Slowly but surely it's returning. I'll tell you what. I've told everyone to keep quiet about your past—make you remember on your own. Maybe I was wrong. Maybe people should tell you what your past was like. If you had been told up front about who Jonathan is, and about your life, maybe it wouldn't have caused such a strong reaction. From now on"—he looked at David and Alice—"you can answer her questions. Don't give her more than she can handle. And give her facts only, not opinions, please."

"I'll give her facts," said a new voice from the hall. "She is a manipulative, conniving woman who trapped David into marriage because this family has money, and she's trash looking for an easy way out."

"Mother!" David turned to the woman in the doorway. "That is not helpful at all."

"But it's the truth, and Doctor Means said to tell her the truth." The woman who spoke to Marnie the night she arrived approached the bed where she sat, cross-legged. "He was engaged to a lovely young woman, a woman of his own class, until you seduced him and got yourself pregnant so he would marry you to give his son a name. If Jonathan didn't look so much like David at that age I would swear he was another man's child. You have certainly had your share of the men in this town, both before and after you married my son."

Chapter 8

"That isn't helpful, Mother."

"Why not? You want her to remember, don't you? She should remember how much she hurt this family. She should remember how much she hurt her husband and child. She should remember how she stole from the company. She should remember all of it."

"No, no," Marnie moaned. "I'm not that kind of person. I'm not. I know I'm not."

"Yes. Yes, you are that very person."

Doctor Means observed Marnie during this accusation. Finally, he put a stop to it.

"Ruth, that's enough. We'll get to the bottom of this memory loss soon enough. For now, I agree with David. This isn't helpful."

The older woman gave one last venomous glance toward the weeping woman in the bed before leaving the room.

"Well, that made a believer out of me," David said.

The doctor looked at him quizzically. "What do you mean?"

"If Marnie was faking this memory loss, she would have lashed back at my mother. She could never keep her mouth shut around her. Marnie put little digs in every sentence she spoke to her. No, Marnie doesn't remember her past. She couldn't have resisted talking back."

"You would know more about that than I would, David. I've got to get to the office. I have patients waiting on me. Young lady," he said, turning to Marnie, "you are growing stronger every day. Start involving yourself in life again. Go downstairs.

When you feel like it, get out of the house. Something will jog your memory, much like the dinosaurs have. Perhaps it will be something more meaningful than a toy next time."

He picked up his bag and started toward the door then turned back to face her. "It may be hard, but try to keep those emotions from overwhelming you again. Now that you've heard the worst from Ruth, steel yourself when you hear what people have to say. Listen for the familiar in what they tell you. If it hurts you to hear about the person you are—or were— maybe that's a good thing. Change is possible, you know."

With those words, he left. David followed him out of the room.

"Now you just lean back and rest," Alice said, fluffing the pillows behind Marnie.

"No, Alice. I had already made up my mind to go downstairs this morning. Do you think it's too late to get some breakfast? I can fix it myself"—she got off the bed and started toward the door then paused—"if someone shows me where the kitchen is."

"Of course you can have some breakfast. You just go on downstairs. Your nose will direct you toward the kitchen. Cook, that is, Mrs. Grady, is baking this morning. I'll be down after I make the bed and tidy up a bit."

"Alice, I'm going to start making the bed myself and cleaning the bathroom. I need something to do to keep busy."

Alice paused in her work and stared at Marnie. "Land sakes! I never thought I'd hear you say that!"

"Why? Don't I do anything to help around the house?"

"No. No, you don't."

"Then what do I do with my time?"

"Well, I never really knew what you did. You usually left the house first thing and stayed gone all day. Shopping mostly, I guess."

"Hmm. That doesn't seem like a good way to keep busy." She had another thought. "Didn't I have a job?"

"Not since you married Mr. David."

Just then Marnie's stomach growled, and she smiled. "I guess I'd better go get some food in me."

Alice chuckled. "Well, if your stomach is any sign, I'd say you are getting better."

"You know, Alice, I do feel better after that cry. I felt so horrible when that spell swept over me, but it's like the tears washed cobwebs away from my brain. Maybe I'll start remembering now."

Marnie descended the wide staircase, seeing the downstairs for the first time since Alice helped her to her bedroom that first day. The expansive foyer was crafted with ornate woodwork and a patterned hardwood floor, but it was as gloomy and depressing as the upstairs. Evidently the last redecorating had been done several decades ago when dark colors and flocked wallpaper were in style.

Since Ruth spoke of being a wealthy family, it seemed to Marnie she ought to spend some money on redecorating. She wondered if that was something they had fought over.

I need to start thinking of her as my mother-in-law. This must be her home, not David's and mine. If it were mine, it would be different. There would be bright colors, and the drapes would be drawn back to let in the sunshine. Maybe I'd do away with drapes altogether. I'll bet I was miserable living in this gloom with a mother-in-law who hates me.

Marnie stood in the foyer at the foot of the carpeted staircase, her hand on the massive walnut newel post. To her left, through an arch, appeared to be the living room, although she doubted much living was done there. She entered the large room and looked around at the space that was as dreary and morose as the bedroom she had been sleeping in and as out-of-date as the other rooms she had seen. Furnished with massive pieces upholstered in dark colors, it did not encourage anyone to stop and stay a while. It smelled musty, as if no one had set foot in it for a long while. If it were hers, she would have thrown open the windows and let fresh air sweep the scent of spring into the room.

She returned to the foyer and entered the room on the other side. The dining room was as antiquated and gloomy as the living room, with a table large enough to seat a formal meal. A sideboard stood against one wall with an ornate silver tea service resting on it. Hanging just above the sideboard was a painting of a couple in formal attire. Marnie studied it, thinking the people looked familiar.

Of course! The woman is Ruth when she was younger, and the man looks like David. It must be a portrait of David's parents.

She surveyed the room and noticed an arched doorway on the back wall that opened into a hall. As she reached it, David entered through a set of swinging doors. He had a muffin in one hand and a cup in the other.

"Oh, hi," he said, as he swallowed a mouthful. "I was just leaving for the office."

The words were said in a pleasant tone, not like the one he had been using.

"What office? That is, what do you do?"

He looked stunned. "Oh, uh, the family owns Barrett Manufacturing. I'm the president and CEO."

"That's your last name then? Barrett? And mine, too?"

"Yes. Barrett. Our name is Barrett."

"I thought so. Some woman, a pretty blonde, called me Mrs. Barrett. I hadn't thought about it until now."

"That was Celeste, I imagine. She was helping with Jonathan while Mrs. Tucker was away."

"Who is Mrs. Tucker?"

"Jonathan's nanny." He waved the cup in the air as he spoke. "Look, I need to get to the office now, but I'll try to get away early today. We can talk when I get home this afternoon. Doctor Means said to answer your questions. Maybe something I tell you will strike a chord and help you to start remembering again. It really is very important you recall the time just before you disappeared."

"How long was I gone?"

His eyes widened as he stared at her. "Wow! I didn't realize you didn't even know that. Almost a month."

"That long?"

"Yes. Well, we'll talk this afternoon. I promise."

She watched as he went down the hall a few steps.

"Look, my mother's suite is down this hall. If you're wandering around today, it's probably best you don't go down there. I'll show you the rooms in that part of the house later."

"OK."

"On the other side of the living room are the library and some other rooms. And there's a garden room at the end of that hall. You can go that way."

"I will. Thank you. I'm just going to get some breakfast now."

"Mrs. Gravy . . . er, Mrs. Grady will fix you up. Bye."

"Bye."

She stared at his tall figure as he strode down the hallway. *This man is my husband. I must have held him in my arms, loved him, kissed him. Yet he seems like a stranger to me. I'm ready for this empty feeling to go away.*

Chapter 9

Marnie watched David disappear through a door in the hallway. She marveled at the fact that his presence always evoked emotion, even though she could not remember their life together. Their relationship puzzled her. There was no doubt he was angry with her, and before today, he did not believe that she had lost her memory. Even then, his presence made her tingle from her scalp to her toes. She was ever-conscious of his presence when they were in the same room and was mesmerized when his eyes were fastened on her. Though she had been hurt by his disbelief, she still caught herself trying to remember what it must have been like to have him kiss her, hold her, make love to her.

Laying those thoughts aside, she pushed open the swinging door and entered the kitchen. As out-of-date as the rest of the house was, the kitchen was up-to-date and well organized. Two walls held modern white cabinets with granite countertops. A six-burner range stood ready for use, and a large granite-topped island with stools on two sides filled the center of the room. A large stainless steel refrigerator stood ajar while a woman looked for something inside.

"What's the matter, Mr. David? You need another muffin to tide you over till lunch? Come back for another one, has ye?" Her voice was tinged with a faint British accent. Closing the door, she turned to see Marnie standing in the doorway. "Oh, good morning, Miss Marnie."

"Good morning," Marnie said awkwardly. "Mrs. . . . . Grady, is it?"

"Mrs. Grady, yes," she answered as she held a bowl

of eggs and a package of butter. She was a woman whose ample, apron-wrapped figure advertised her cooking skills. Her hair was a shade of red that only came from a bottle. She looked as if she didn't know what to say.

"I didn't quite understand David when he told me your name. You've heard, I guess, that I have amnesia and don't remember anything about my life."

"I heard that, yes. My goodness, we've all been talking about it." No longer caught by surprise, the cook's words flowed. "Mr. David probably called me Mrs. Gravy, didn't he?"

"Er, yes, he did. Then he said Mrs. Grady. I wasn't too sure about it."

"He was just a little tyke when I came to work for the Barretts, and he thought my name was Mrs. Gravy. He learned the right of it when he got older, but he still calls me Mrs. Gravy. It's our little joke, it is."

She set the items on the island. "You're a bit hungry, I wouldn't doubt. Want me to whip you up some eggs? Or pancakes, maybe?"

"I don't want to cause you extra work, Mrs. Grady. I can see you were getting ready to bake something. I can fix my own breakfast."

"It's no trouble, dearie, no trouble at all. If you like, you can have one of my blueberry muffins. Mr. David is fond of them."

"That sounds wonderful. With a glass of milk, perhaps?"

Mrs. Grady fetched a tumbler from a glass-paned cabinet and went back to the refrigerator for milk.

"And are you remembering anything? Anything at all?"

"No. Not really. Thank you," Marnie said as Mrs. Grady placed a glass of milk and a plate with a muffin on it before her. "Mm. Blueberry," she said with a mouthful. "Delicious."

"I put me up plenty of blueberries in the freezer, I did. Last summer it was. Mr. David especially likes 'em, and I wanted enough to last till next summer." She sat on a stool at the island and began peeling apples that sat in a large bowl.

"I'm making my apple cake. It'll be ready for supper. Lunch'll be in a couple of hours. Mrs. Ruth and Miss Celeste are eating at the club—the country club, that is—so it's soup and sandwiches for Mrs. Tucker and Jonathan—and you, of course."

"That'll be fine with me. I don't want to put you out any."

"Won't put me out none. I keep soup in the freezer, too. I can heat up how much I need at the drop of a hat. Days when nobody is home, I spend putting up extra."

"I haven't met Mrs. Tucker yet." She thought it better not to mention she had met Jonathan but hadn't known he was her son until this morning.

"You haven't . . . er . . . no, I guess you don't remember her, either."

"David said she is Jonathan's nanny, and she has been gone. Someone named Celeste has been taking care of Jonathan?" she asked.

"You might say that," Mrs. Grady replied enigmatically. "Mrs. Tucker's sister passed away, and she had to go be with her in her last days and make arrangements. Miss Celeste is an old friend of the family who volunteered to stay and watch after Jonathan." She sniffed loudly, giving the impression she didn't care for the situation.

Marnie didn't want to get into a gossip session with the cook, although she had no doubt she could be greatly informed and entertained by the woman's tales if she so chose.

"Thank you for the delicious muffin, Mrs. Grady. I'll just wash these dishes. Then I'm going to explore this floor of the house. I'm hoping something will trigger my memory, get my mind to recall my past."

"No need to wash them, dearie. Just put them in the sink, and I'll load them into the dishwasher when I put my bowls in. Thank you for offering, though. That was very thoughtful of you, it was.

"Now, mind you, don't go down the east hall. That's the

hall to the right past the swinging door. Mrs. Ruth's rooms are that way. She's not home, but it's best you don't go there. Go to the living room—you can find that, can't you? Go into the west hall and you can go into any of the rooms that way."

"Thank you, Mrs. Grady."

"Lord love us. Isn't it something? You not remembering anything. Not your husband, not your sweet little boy, none of us who work here."

Marnie thought it was best to avoid a conversation about her memory, so she smiled and left. She retraced her steps through the dining room and foyer. In the living room, she noticed an arched doorway on the back wall that was similar to the one in the dining room.

Marnie could see a room at the far end of the west hall that was separated from the rest of the house by etched-glass French doors. As she made her way down the hall, she opened doors as she came to them. She discovered a powder room and a storage closet before she entered a large, sunlit room furnished with overstuffed furniture covered in colorful striped fabric. A baby grand piano stood in one corner, but a couple of chairs made it inaccessible. A table and four chairs stood in front of tall windows overlooking the backyard.

I must have liked this room, she thought. *It's the first friendly room I've seen in this house. I'll bet I spent a lot of time in this den.*

Marnie explored the doors and drawers that covered one wall. When she opened the middle set of doors, she found a big screen television, below which were rows of DVDs and VHS movies. She wondered if she and David watched movies here together, and if Ruth joined them.

The next set of doors revealed an old stereo system and vinyl records alongside tapes and CDs. Behind the final set of doors were shelves full of games of every description. Everything necessary for a pleasant evening at home could be found there.

After leaving that room, Marnie continued down the hall to a door on the opposite side. Decorated in dark colors, it somehow was not as gloomy as the living room or dining room. Deep green walls peaked out from behind bookcases full of books of all genres. In front of the fireplace stood two leather chairs, and over the fireplace was a man's portrait. He resembled the man in the portrait Marnie had seen hanging in the dining room. She surmised it might be David's grandfather. A grand mahogany desk rested on a vibrant oriental rug.

After choosing a book to read later, she tucked it under her arm and proceeded down the hall toward the French doors at the end, skipping other doors along the way. There she found a sizable, sunlit room with windows on three sides that overlooked the snow-covered yard. Another set of French doors on the back wall opened onto a patio.

The space was furnished with white-painted wicker furniture, the pads of which were covered in bright floral and striped fabric. Once again, Marnie was amazed at the difference between the dark, gloomy areas of the house and the comfortable, friendly salons she had discovered today.

She surveyed the room for a couple of minutes and imagined how much nicer it would look if it had some green plants to fill the space.

It is beautiful in here, but it's too cool for me to sit and read, she thought, *at least in winter.*

She traced her steps back to the pleasant room she thought of as the den. Settling into a comfortable overstuffed chair, she drew her feet up under her and began to read. Within a few minutes, the events of the morning—the news that Jonathan was her son and she had not been a good mother to him, the crying spell, David's seeming acceptance of her memory loss, exploring the home she still did not remember—caught up with her. The words on the page blurred, the book lowered to her lap, and she fell asleep.

She awoke to find the same dark-haired handsome man sitting in a chair, staring at her, frowning, just like her first memory of him.

Chapter 10

"I must have fallen asleep. How long have you been sitting there?"

"A few minutes. I see you've been reading."

"Yes, I found the library. I remembered as I was looking through the books that I like certain authors. I must have read these before."

He frowned again. "Not that I can recall," he said briefly.

"I'm sure I must have liked this room. It's so sunny and comfortable, not like some rooms in the house."

"You do complain a lot about the house."

"Well, this room is nice, so are the library and sunroom at the end of this hall. Surely I spent a lot of time in them. Do we sit in here to watch TV or listen to music?"

"No. You listen to music on your iPod."

"Oh."

He looked thoughtful. "Come to think of it, wherever you were, you must have left your purse and your iPod. You had them when you went missing and didn't when you came back."

"I had a purse over my arm. I looked in it to try to find something with my name and address on it."

"You have a lot of purses. You always have a billfold and makeup wherever you go. And your cell phone, of course. There wasn't much in the one you came home with."

"I know."

He stood up. "Let's go out for lunch. Mrs. Grady has already fed Mrs. Tucker and Jonathan. Go upstairs and get a coat."

She scrambled to her feet. "Are jeans good enough, or do I need to change?"

"Jeans are fine. Just get a coat. It's cold out."

When Marnie returned to the foyer, David was waiting for her. Without a word, he went through the dining room and turned into the east hall. Marnie followed, slightly miffed that he didn't speak but obviously expected her to keep up. She reckoned his dismissive attitude toward her might be part of the trouble between them.

When they reached the door he had disappeared through earlier, she saw it led to a large garage. A silver BMW and a red Mustang were parked in two of the spaces. Marnie presumed Ruth parked her car in the empty spot. David had started for the driver's side of the BMW when he noticed she was still standing in the doorway. He corrected his direction and opened the passenger door for her.

"Thank you," she murmured as she slid onto the soft leather seat. She breathed in the aroma of new leather as he slipped into the driver's seat and started the engine. It roared to life, and he backed out onto what appeared to be a courtyard.

As they drove, Marnie noticed the houses she had walked by a week earlier. When they reached Main Street, David turned right, taking them on a new route.

I must have driven this way before, she thought.

"Anything look familiar?" he asked, just as she was thinking it didn't.

"No, nothing."

They went around a square with a courthouse in the middle. On the far side, David pointed out a shop. "That's Nicole's, your favorite place to shop. You buy something there at least once a week."

"That's where the receipt in my pocket was from, the one with the address on it."

He nodded. "Yes, I know. I would have thought you'd remember it."

"Well, if I can't remember you and Jonathan and the house I live in, I doubt I'd remember a dress shop."

He shrugged and guided the car away from the town square, down a street filled with businesses that changed character as they progressed. Quaint antique shops, clothing stores, boutiques, and flower shops evolved into auto parts stores, pawnshops, and thrift stores. After another mile, he pulled into a parking lot. A gaudy neon sign proclaimed the place to be the Roadhouse Café. Other neon signs advertising various brands of beer plastered the exterior walls. It looked fairly disreputable, and Marnie wondered why he brought her there.

They entered the large room, and they were assailed with the smell of cigarette smoke and stale beer. She looked around at the dark-paneled walls, covered with posters and signs advertising beer, rodeos, and wrestling matches. A jukebox on the far wall was playing a twangy country song as a waitress in short shorts and a tight tee shirt approached them.

"Well, look who the cat drug in!"

"Hello, Jolene," David responded.

"Sit anywhere you like, hon. No one much here middle of the afternoon."

David directed Marnie to a booth on the back wall, well away from the other customers.

"How you been, Marnie? You look kinda peaked."

"Um, I've had the flu," she said. "Chills and fever." She didn't know how else answer, since she certainly wasn't going to get into a conversation about her memory loss with a waitress in a beer joint, even if she did know her name.

"It's sure goin' 'round bad. Can I get you folks some beers?"

David looked at Marnie and raised his eyebrows in question.

"I'll have a Coke, please."

"Sure thing, hon. How 'bout you, Mr. Barrett?"

"I'll take a beer. Draft," he answered.

Marnie watched the woman make her way back to the bar, where a heavyset man was drying glasses and placing them on a shelf in front of a mirrored wall.

"What are you thinking?" David asked.

"I was wondering how long she had to practice to learn how to wiggle her buns like that," Marnie replied.

David cracked up.

Marnie grinned. "It's not that funny," she said as he continued to chuckle.

"What's funny is that you swing your tushie a hell of a lot better than Jolene does."

"I do?" She couldn't think of anything to say after a statement like that.

Jolene returned with their drinks. "You ready to order?"

"Hamburger with everything . . . and fries," David answered. He looked at Marnie. "Is that OK?"

She nodded in agreement.

"Comin' right up."

"I take it I've been here before, since Jolene knows me."

"You might say that."

Marnie was getting thoroughly ticked off at his enigmatic answers, and her voice was sharp as she countered. "Well, why don't you say that, then? How about helping me out here? Did we eat here often?"

"No. We didn't eat here. At least we didn't after we married. Jolene knows you because you worked here."

She fell back against the red vinyl seat. "I worked here?"

"Yep. Wiggled your cute little tushie at me . . . till you caught me." His voice turned bitter, and he took a swig from the frothy mug in front of him.

"I . . . I wore clothes like that?" she glanced at Jolene who was standing at the bar.

"Nope, yours were shorter and tighter."

"I was a waitress, in a place like this." It was a statement, not a question. She looked him square in the eyes and asked, "What did I do here?"

He leaned across the table until his face almost touched hers. In a low, sexy voice, he answered, "Anything you could, sweetheart. Anything you could."

Chapter 11

At first, the meaning of his words floated by her. *Surely, he didn't mean what it sounded like,* she thought. His smirk and his stare revealed the cold, hard truth. *Yes, he meant it all right. But I couldn't have. I just couldn't have. No way am I the woman he is implying.*

Ever since Ruth had faced her on the stairs that first day and told her she was going to jail, Marnie had worried about what she could have done, what kind of person she was. This morning she had faced the fact she was a bad mother, and Ruth had said she was an unfaithful wife. Now she was being told she was promiscuous. David didn't have to spell it out. What he meant was plain.

She closed her eyes to steady herself against the spinning sensation.

I will not pass out. I will not pass out, she repeated as she gripped the edge of the table tightly.

"Marnie? What's the matter?" His voice was suddenly concerned.

He got up and moved to her side of the booth and put his arm around her.

"Hang on. Don't faint. Here, take a sip of your drink." He held the glass to her lips.

She took a sip. After a minute, she opened her eyes. The room had stopped spinning.

"Are you OK? You turned so white and were holding on so tightly I thought you were going to pass out."

"I'll be OK in a minute. What you said . . . it shook me, that's all. I don't like what I'm finding out about myself."

At that point, Jolene appeared with their order.

"Marnie, you all right? You're as white as a sheet."

"She'll be OK. This is the first time she's been out of the house since she was ill. She'll feel better when she eats something."

Marnie drank some more of her Coke and ate a French fry. "I feel better." As David withdrew his arm, she couldn't help but feel disappointed.

She sat up and reached for her hamburger. Taking a big bite, she made a face as she chewed it and swallowed. Pulling the top off, she looked on the table where the catsup was sitting.

"Is everything good? Do you need anything else?" Jolene asked.

"Yes, I need some mustard," Marnie said.

"Well, my mistake. I thought you took mayo on your burger," Jolene said. She returned quickly with a yellow squeeze bottle.

David watched Marnie take her hamburger apart and use her knife to scrape the mayonnaise off the bun and the meat. "Since when did you change from mayo to mustard?" he asked.

"I don't know," she answered sharply. "I evidently don't know anything at all about myself. I would have said I like children and would be a good mother. Wrong. I would have said I was a faithful wife. Wrong. I would say I've always liked mustard on my hamburger. Wrong. I can't imagine what's next." She sighed heavily as she reassembled the now-acceptable burger. "I only hope it's more like the last thing instead of the first two. I can't take many more surprises like those."

They ate in silence for a while and then Marnie spoke. "So, I worked here. Is this where we met?"

"Yes, but I think I'd rather talk about that when we get home. I'd like more privacy when we discuss it."

"Why? Are you afraid I'm going to throw another crying fit like I did this morning?"

"Maybe. Mostly I just don't want anyone overhearing us."

"I'm finished and ready to go any time you are," she told him.

He took out his wallet and tossed a few bills on the table. "Let's go."

They took a different route back. She thought he was testing her memory, trying to show her places she might remember, or that he was trying to get her to blurt out something that would prove she was faking her amnesia. After a few minutes, she saw they were on the street by the park where her memories started.

"Wait, David." She placed her hand on his arm. "I remember this. Right there," she pointed at a small copse of leafless trees. "I was standing there. The rain stung my cheeks. That's the first thing I remember." He pulled over to the curb. "I crossed the street here and walked down to the next corner."

"Think hard. Can you remember anything before that? Where you were? Where had you been? It's important, Marnie. You took something when you left, and it's important that I get it back, if it's not too late. Where were you before this park?"

"I don't know. I've tried and tried to remember, but I can't. Believe me, David, this is not fun, not fun at all. I would remember if I could."

He turned off the engine. "Let's walk up on the slope to where you were standing. Maybe your billfold and iPod are buried under the leaves, or maybe being there again will jog your memory."

They searched through the snow-covered leaves to no avail. There was no sign Marnie had been there before. The snow was still covering a good portion of the ground, and although some of it had melted, objects might still be hidden from sight.

"I remember how I felt when I discovered I didn't know who I was. It felt like someone had punched me in the stomach . . . hard. Everything was spinning, and I had to hold onto a tree to stay standing." He put his arm around her and pulled her closer, as if he thought she might have the same reaction now.

"Let's go back to the car," he suggested. "We need to come back and look again when all the snow is gone."

When they were in the car being warmed by the heater, he asked, "Where did you go next?"

"I walked down to that corner"—she pointed—"and I turned left."

He put the car in gear and followed her directions.

"I looked in that café and thought about going in, but I had looked in my purse by then and knew I didn't even have enough money for a cup of coffee. I thought about going in and asking if anyone knew me or knew where I lived, but I was too embarrassed to do that."

David's face was serious, but his look was different than before. She thought maybe he was beginning to believe her.

"What then?"

"I put my hands in my coat pockets and found the receipt from Nicole's. It had the address on it, and when I walked a bit farther"—she waved her hand to the front and David inched the car on down the street—"I saw that street sign, so I walked until I came to 1532. I couldn't have gone another step."

"Alice said she was vacuuming by the window in my bedroom when she saw you coming up the drive and rushed out to meet you."

"If she hadn't, I probably would have passed out right there in the drive."

"Well, she did, and you're home safe and sound."

"I guess I'm safe enough, but sound is another matter. Mentally I don't feel so sound," she said. "David, am I going crazy?"

Chapter 12

"I don't think you're crazy, Marnie. I will admit I thought you were pretending to have amnesia."

"Why would I do that?"

"To get out of trouble. To avoid your involvement in a theft of property. To pretend you didn't know what had happened. To get me to forgive you, once again. Who knows?"

"Do you still think I'm pretending?"

"Let's say I still have doubts about your truthfulness, but if you're acting, you're doing a darn good job of it."

"I'm not pretending. I really don't remember anything before waking up in that park."

"I want to believe you. The question now is what happened to cause you to lose your memory? It must have been pretty traumatic."

"I wish I knew. If I knew what happened, maybe the rest of it would come back."

She thought about all she had discovered so far that day. It was more than she had learned the whole prior week. From David, she found out Jonathan was her son and she had ignored him for much of his life. From Ruth, she had learned she had gotten pregnant in order to get David to marry her, that she had stolen something from the family company, and that she was promiscuous before and after marriage. David confirmed that fact when he described her behavior at the Roadhouse.

Besides all these revelations, she had explored the house where she lived and found several rooms where she felt at home, and found books she liked and had probably read.

She had experienced an emotional breakdown when told she was Jonathan's neglectful mother, but when she recovered from that crying spell, she felt better and more clear-headed than at any other time since she found herself in the park. She finally felt like she was stronger and ready to solve the mystery of what had happened to her.

"The worst thing—the very worst—isn't the fact I can't remember anything, nor even the possibility I may never get those memories back. The worst thing is knowing I'm a bad person."

"I don't know that I would say you're a bad person. I would say you behave badly . . . very badly."

"Only a bad person would neglect her son and cheat on her husband. And evidently, from what you've said, I was what? Promiscuous?"

"All that and more," came his terse reply.

"I don't want to be that person. If recalling my past means going back to that life, I'll do without it."

"I keep thinking about a guy I knew in college," David said. "Between our sophomore and junior years he was in a horrific car wreck. He was in a coma for a month. When he woke up, he said he had died and gone to heaven. He said he had looked down on his body in the emergency room and then went toward a beautiful light. He saw his grandparents who had died earlier and a friend from his childhood who had drowned. They told him it wasn't his time to die, but he had to straighten out his life and be a better person. Sometime after that, he woke up in the hospital bed."

"Really? I think I've read about cases like that, but I never knew if they were true or not."

"Up until then, he had been a real goof-off. He got drunk a lot. He cut classes, paid people to write his papers for him, slept around."

"Did he change?"

"Yeah, he sure did. He turned into a fine man. He

stopped drinking and pulled his grades up all on his own. He graduated, not with honors, but with decent grades."

"So, there's hope for me. Is that what you're saying?"

"I'm saying he was different when he came back to school. You're different, too. That is, you're you, but you're not. Do you understand what I'm saying?"

"Not really."

"Well, you're still Marnie, but you haven't groused one time about being stuck in the house, and you hate that house. You seem to really like Jonathan—"

"I do. I do like Jonathan," she interrupted, "but I still don't like the house."

"You spend time with him, which you never did before."

Marnie turned her head and looked out the car window, vowing not to cry.

"I'm concerned that when your memory returns you'll go back to ignoring him, and he will be hurt even more by your indifference, after having had your attention."

She wanted to promise she wouldn't return to her old self but hesitated to make that pledge. She had no assurance of what she would be like if and when the amnesia was gone.

"You haven't said anything about money or wanting to buy anything in the days you've been back. That's unusual for you. And you're dressing differently."

"Dressing differently? But I'm wearing the clothes I found in my closet."

"Yes, but you're putting them together in a different way. Take what you're wearing, for example. You might wear those tight jeans, but you'd put a skin-tight tee shirt with them, one short enough to show your belly button. And you might leave your bra off."

Marnie took a deep breath and put her hands over her navel, even though it was covered with layers of cloth. "Oh," she said.

"So now I'm wondering what could have happened to

you to change you so much, like it changed the guy I knew in college. Doctor Means says you don't seem to have been in an accident of any kind. At least you don't have any broken bones or bruises to show for it, but I keep thinking you must have had some sort of life-altering event to be acting so differently."

They pulled into the circle drive in front of the house, pulling up behind a black Mercedes. David sighed.

"Whose car is that?" she asked.

"It's Celeste's."

"The woman who was taking care of Jonathan?"

"In a way. When Mrs. Tucker had to leave unexpectedly, Celeste volunteered to help, said it was too much for my mother to handle. I don't know how much taking care of Jonathan Celeste actually did. Probably Alice, Mary, and Mrs. Gravy did most of it."

They had gotten out of the car and started up the front steps when the door opened and the attractive blonde exited the house.

"Hello, darling," she said, taking David by the arm and kissing him on the cheek. She smiled warmly as she took her finger and wiped off the lipstick she had left on his skin. "Hello, Marnie," she said, her eyes never leaving David's face.

"Hello, Celeste," David answered. "Just leaving?"

"Yes. I do so enjoy spending time with your mother, but I think she needs to rest a while. We've been making a day of it. She's invited me for supper, but I don't know whether to come back or not. Should I?"

She's making a blatant play for my husband! Marnie thought. *Even if I don't remember he's my husband, that's not a nice thing to do, and I don't like it!*

"Marnie and I just finished a late lunch, Celeste, so I don't imagine we'll want much supper. Feel free to join Mother at the table if you want to, but if she's tired, she may want to eat in her room." He took Marnie by the arm and started through the open door.

Celeste gave a tight smile. "Fine. Another time, perhaps," she said and continued down the steps to her car.

When they were inside with the door closed, Marnie turned to David and asked, "Who is Celeste to you?"

"She's who I was engaged to when I married you."

Chapter 13

Astounded, Marnie questioned further, "You were engaged to someone else when we married?" Suddenly, she remembered that Ruth had mentioned it when she confronted her earlier.

"Let's go up to your room and discuss this in private," David said as he took her by the arm. Just then his cell phone rang, and he pulled it out of his pocket.

As he talked, Marnie thought, *My room? Why isn't it our room? Where is he sleeping?* She wondered if he had been sharing a room with Celeste, if his ex-fiancée had been living in the house while she supposedly cared for Jonathan. Jealousy started edging its way into her brain.

Ridiculous, she thought. *Absolutely ridiculous to be jealous of a man I feel like I just met.* As quickly as she had that thought, another popped into her head. *He's my husband. Whether I remember him or not, I have every right to be jealous.*

After a few words, he turned to her. "We'll have to put off our talk for now. I need to go back to the plant. I promise we'll talk at the first opportunity."

She was filled with questions but acquiesced. "OK," she said quietly.

He tipped her chin up with his finger. "That's another way you've changed. I'd have expected you to throw a hissy fit when I put off talking to you. It's like you've grown up, become more adult. Maybe whatever happened to you was a good thing."

Marnie looked into his deep blue eyes. For a minute, she thought he was going to kiss her, but at last he removed his finger and broke eye contact. Striding to the front door, he turned and smiled before opening it. "Bye," he said and was gone.

When she returned to her room, she found Alice putting fresh towels in the bathroom.

"You seem like you're doing a lot better today, Miss Marnie. I was lookin' for you earlier, to be sure you were OK, and Cook said you and Mr. David went out for lunch."

"Yes, he took me to the Roadhouse."

Alice said nothing, but the look on her face registered disapproval.

"He told me I used to work there. I think he was hoping that going there would bring up some memories."

"Did it?"

"No, it didn't." Marnie went to one of the armchairs in front of the window and sat down. "Alice, David told me you have known me since I was a little girl."

"Yes, that's right."

"Since the doctor has said people can tell me some things about my past, would you come sit with me and visit? Please? I have to get some clue about why I am the person David and Ruth say I am. They are painting a terrible picture of the things I've done."

Alice went to the chair facing Marnie and sat down. "Ever since you came home with no memory, I've been thinking a lot about those days and what you were like then."

"Tell me. What was I like?"

"You were just a little girl when you and your mother moved in across the hall from me. That was in the Green Oaks Apartments over on Poplar Street. She and your papa had just gotten a divorce."

"My parents! You know, Alice, in all this trouble, I haven't given any thought to my mother and father. Does she still live here? Where is my father?"

"No, honey. She died about five or six years ago. I don't know nothin' about your papa, whether he's still alive or not. I never knew him. I think he lived in Phoenix. She mentioned that one time."

"I'm sorry I interrupted. Please go on."

"Anyway, Pamela had just gotten a divorce and a job. I don't remember right off where you moved here from, Phoenix maybe, but she got a job as secretary to Mr. Robert Barrett, David's father, and moved here. Like I said, she moved in right across the hall. I was already working here in this house. I've been a maid here since I was old enough to work. I was part time when I was in high school, helping out with parties and such. When I graduated, I had a job working at the five and dime, but when another maid quit, I came to work here and I've been here ever since.

"That sort of made a connection between me and Pamela, both working for the same folks. Of course, she was in a different class from me. She was real high class, always dressed to the nines, she was, and I'm just working folk."

Marnie leaned forward and rested her forearms on her legs. "What did she look like, Alice? Do I look like her?"

"No, you don't. Well, maybe I'm wrong about that. You have her chin and mouth. But her coloring was different. She kept her hair blond, but I think her natural color was light brown. That's what color her eyebrows were, and that's usually how you tell. You must have gotten your dark hair and eyes from your papa."

"This is so interesting, Alice. Thank you for sharing." She leaned back in the chair. "Did I ever get to see my father?"

"Not that I ever knew, and I think I'd know. I'd baby-sit you when your mother went out, which wasn't very often, or when she had to work late, which she did a lot. You'd come across the hall to my place or else I'd go across to yours. She and I were friends, but she didn't tell me her personal stuff."

"Doctor Means said I was always getting scrapes and bruises when I was a kid."

Alice laughed. "Yes, you were. You was never interested in playing dolls with the other girls in the neighborhood. You followed the boys instead, on your bike or roller skates. At that age, they'd try to avoid you or run you off, but you were a persistent little thing. You tried your best to keep up."

"The doctor told me I broke my arm when I was ten trying to get into their treehouse."

Alice gave another chuckle. "Yes, I remember that time. The boys had a treehouse in that great big oak tree in the vacant lot next to the apartment house. You were forever trying to get in there, and they were forever stopping you. So, one day you decided to climb up the tree next to it, shimmy along a branch that reached over to where you wanted to go, and get in the treehouse that way. Trouble was, the branch broke and down you came. You ended up with a broke arm."

"It seems like I would remember something like a broken arm." Marnie rubbed first one arm, then the other, as if that would bring back a memory.

"Anyway, you always did like to be where the boys were. When you was a little thing, it was funny, but when you got to be a teenager, it was a problem. You liked the boys, and the boys liked you—too much, if you get my meaning.

"When you graduated from high school, your mother promised you a new car if you'd go to business school in Centerview and graduate with good grades. She thought you needed good training so's you could always find work. She said she was living proof a woman needed to be able to support herself."

"It sounds like she had a hard life and wanted me to be able to take care of myself."

"Yes, she did, but Pamela always did spoil you rotten—bought you new clothes and whatever you wanted. But she didn't have enough money to give you everything the rich kids had, and that's what you wanted—to be rich and go dancing at the country club and swimming in the club pool in the summer."

Marnie got to her feet and walked to the other side of the room. "It sounds like I was more interested in the things money could buy, rather than being sure I had a way to earn my own living. Did I go to business school?"

"You finished business school, all right, and got your car—a red convertible you drove all over town. Your mother was set on you doing something you could make a living at. She said she didn't get enough alimony and child support to get by, but she had a good job. You got a job right off, at an architect's office, but you didn't like it. You said it was 'boring as all get out' and you wanted to work where the action was. When you turned twenty-one, you quit and went to work at the Roadhouse. You said you could make more in tips than you could being a secretary. But that's an awful rough place to work."

"Is that where I met David?"

"You might have met him there. I don't know. But that's not where you were when you started dating. You were working at Barrett Enterprises."

"Where my mother worked?"

"Well, see, she had a heart attack and died, all of a sudden. I don't think she even knew she had any heart problems. And about the same time, you got fired at the Roadhouse."

"Why did I get fired?"

"Sam's wife—Sam Whiteville is the owner—Sam's wife said you were carrying on with Sam and threatened to leave him if he didn't fire you, so he did."

"Was I? Carrying on with Sam?"

"I don't know for sure. You were young and pretty, and Sam was middle-aged and fat. You could have had anyone you wanted. I don't know why you'd want Sam. But maybe there was some advantage to it. You were always looking out for what or who could give you something."

Marnie shook her head in denial. The more she heard, the less she liked herself.

"So there you was, your mother dead and you with no job. So Mr. Robert offered you a job at the plant."

"I got my mother's job?"

Alice chuckled. "Land's no, child. She had years of experience, and you didn't. He got you a job in one of the offices—I don't know which one. I think you set your sights on Mr. David at that point. You'd see him in the plant and come home saying how handsome he was. He'd finished college by then and was being trained by his father and his Uncle John about how everything at the plant worked."

"David said he was engaged to Celeste when we got married. How did that happen?"

"Yes, he was engaged to Miss Celeste. Then everything changed."

"How? Why?"

"What changed everything was the plane crash."

Chapter 14

"A plane crash?"

"Yes, Mr. Robert and Mr. John were flying to meet with some government people about some contract for Barrett Enterprises to make something. They were in their own private plane, and a storm came up. Mr. Robert, Mr. John, and the pilot were all killed. That's when Mr. David had to take over the whole business by himself."

"That must have been hard, his being so young and just learning everything."

"It was, and for a while there, he kinda went off and started drinking too much. He was engaged to Miss Celeste, but he started seeing you, too"—Alice stood up—"and then you two got married, and that's all I can tell you."

"This morning Ruth said I had gotten pregnant to trap him into marriage."

"That's between you and Mr. David. It isn't any of my business," Alice said determinedly.

"But you can answer me this. How long had we been married when Jonathan was born?"

After a long pause, Alice answered, "Almost six months."

Alice picked up the pile of dirty towels from where she had put them by the door and left, leaving Marnie with some history of her childhood. It didn't help. She didn't remember any more than she had before the conversation, which was nothing, and it brought up a lot more questions. She wished David would come home and tell her more about how they became involved with each other.

After sitting a while longer, pondering all she had learned, she decided to go see what Jonathan was doing and meet Mrs. Tucker. *Although,* she thought, *I've already met her many times, I'm sure.*

She found them in the playroom. Jonathan was sitting on the floor, running his toy cars over a road he had built of wooden blocks. An older woman sat in the rocking chair, crocheting. Marnie had imagined Mrs. Tucker to be a younger woman, someone who would sit on the floor and play with her son, or throw a ball in the yard, or help him learn to ride a bike. If she, Marnie, had failed to be a good mother, she at least had a vision of a kindly person, perhaps a young widow or divorcée, who could be active with a young child.

The woman who glanced up from her handiwork was, perhaps, in her sixties. She had gray hair, which was pulled back from her face in a tight bun. She looked up at Marnie through round, steel-rimmed glasses and lowered the yarn project to her lap.

"Good evening, Mrs. Barrett."

"Good evening," Marnie answered and looked at Jonathan. "Hello, Jonathan."

"Hi," he replied, smiling at her.

"Say, 'Good evening, Mother'," the older woman prompted.

"Good evening, Mother," he parroted and looked down at his lap. His smile had faded.

Marnie knew at that moment she didn't like Mrs. Tucker. It wasn't that she spoke in an unkind tone, but she could tell in that one brief exchange Mrs. Tucker was a stickler for protocol and preciseness far beyond good manners. In that moment, Marnie determined she would spend more time with her son than she had in her forgotten past, and she would watch Mrs. Tucker to see if she treated Jonathan with love and kindness. The thought of him not being loved almost brought her back to tears, but she held her emotions in check. She didn't dare risk another meltdown.

"Mrs. Tucker, I'm sure someone in the household has told you about my loss of memory."

"Yes. It was explained to me." Mouth set in a firm line, she looked as if she didn't believe any such thing was possible.

"So, you see, it's like this is the first time I've met you."

The older woman sat silently, waiting for more.

"People tell me I was not very involved in my son's life before, but I intend to correct that deficiency. I will be spending more time with Jonathan now."

"Are you firing me?"

"No, not at all. I'm sure Jonathan is very attached to you, and I'm also sure I will not be able to spend all my time with him. You are still needed, but I will be asking questions about his care."

The older woman's face changed as relief washed over her. *Why, she was afraid of losing her job*, Marnie thought.

"How long have you been with Jonathan?"

"Since he was about two weeks old, so that would be a little over four years."

"So you're four, Jonathan?" Marnie asked with a smile.

"Yes, ma'am." He smiled back at her.

"And you do everything with him? Do I do anything for him?"

"I stay with him day and night. I usually have Saturdays and Sundays off, and he goes wherever his father goes. Or that girl, Mary, takes care of him."

"Does he go to any preschool or anything like that?"

"No. His grandmother told me to teach him his ABCs and good manners. She's the one who hired me, not you," she said with a tone of disgust.

Why am I not taking care of my own child? Why is he not in some sort of learning environment? And why is Ruth the person who hired Jonathan's caretaker, not me or David?

"Well, I'm sure you've been doing a good job caring for him. He seems to be a polite and well-behaved young man, and since it sounds like I haven't been spending much time with him, you must be the person responsible for that. Thank you."

With that, Mrs. Tucker smiled, and it seemed to Marnie she relaxed even more.

"You're welcome, Mrs. Barrett. It is a pleasure to care for him. He is a very good little boy, and smart, too."

"The doctor can't tell me when or if my memory will come back, so until it does, I may be asking you some questions—questions I should already know the answers to."

"That's perfectly all right, Mrs. Barrett. You ask away. It must be terrible, losing your memory like that."

At that moment, a buzzer sounded. Marnie looked around and saw the small contraption above the door. Mrs. Tucker provided an explanation.

"That's the signal from the kitchen to indicate our supper is ready." She stood and walked to a button on the wall beside the door. "I buzz back once to let Mrs. Grady know I've heard it and we'll be coming down. If I want it sent up for any reason, if Jonathan is sick, for example, I buzz twice."

"They send it up on the stupid thing!" Jonathan exclaimed.

"The dumbwaiter, Jonathan," Mrs. Tucker corrected him.

"Dumbwaiter," he repeated. "Do you want to see it?"

"Certainly," Marnie answered. "That sounds very interesting."

Jonathan took her hand and led her into the hall to a door a few steps away. Opening it revealed a compartment about two feet wide and two feet deep. On the side was a button similar to an elevator button.

"See, Mrs. Grady puts the tray on the stu—uh, dumbwaiter and pushes the button, and it comes up here to us, and we get it off."

"How very handy that is!"

Mrs. Tucker spoke up. "Not only for meals, but the maids can send the laundry up and down on it also. It makes it easier than carrying it up and down the stairs."

"I can see it would help a lot," Marnie replied.

"Come, Jonathan. You know you must put away your cars and blocks before we go down to eat." She placed her hand on his shoulder. "Say goodnight to your mother before we go."

He looked up into Mrs. Tucker's face and then dropped his gaze to the floor.

"Goodnight, Mother," he intoned.

Chapter 15

Marnie sat and looked out over the moonlit yard. She had pushed and pulled the chair until it faced the windows. The effort left her exhausted, but it felt good to be able to do it at all. Now she was able to relax and admire the moonlight shining on the snow that covered the ground and bushes.

She had mentally catalogued everything that seemed somewhat familiar to her—there wasn't much—and the things she had learned about herself—there was more, but it wasn't flattering. Now she was trying to think of something to keep herself busy tomorrow. She supposed she could retrieve the book she had started reading, but that did not appeal to her. She hoped that when David had time to talk to her he would tell her she had a job somewhere. *Maybe I work at the Barrett business, whatever that is, like Alice said I used to, or maybe I do volunteer work of some sort.* She knew whatever it was she probably wouldn't remember how to do it until her memory came back, but maybe trying would speed up the process.

She thought about spending time with Jonathan. Knowing that nothing could make up for the four years she had ignored him, she was determined to start afresh. She could read to him and play games with him. They could walk through the big house, and he could tell her about things there, perhaps renew her recollection of events that had happened.

The door opened, and she peeked around the side of the wingback chair to see David, illuminated by the light coming from the hallway.

"Hi," said Marnie.

"Oh, there you are. I didn't see you sitting there in the dark."

"You can turn a light on. I was sitting here looking at the moonlight on the snow and thinking."

He turned on the lamp beside her.

"I'm sorry I had to leave so suddenly. Something came up at the plant, and I had to go straighten things out."

"What do you make in the plant?"

"A variety of parts used in aircraft and missiles. Much of it is top secret. We're a small operation, specializing in certain things."

She stood and started to push the chair back to its original position.

"Here, let me do that," he said, and easily did what had taken her several minutes to do earlier. "I thought we could talk now, if that's all right with you."

"Oh, yes! The more I learn, the more questions I have. I visited with Alice earlier this afternoon. She said she has known me since I was a little girl, which you had told me, and that my mother and I lived in the apartment across the hall from her. She said my mother worked for your father."

"Yes, she did."

"Tell me about my mother."

"I don't know much, really. I'm sure Alice knew her better than I did."

"Tell me what you do know."

"She was my father's executive secretary until she died suddenly of a heart attack."

"And she started working for him when I was just a little girl?"

"I guess. I would have been a kid myself then. I'm four years older than you."

"How old am I?"

David stared at her. It was hard to fathom she didn't know the simplest things, like her age.

"You're twenty-eight, and I'm thirty-two."

"Do you know where we lived before we moved here? Alice said we had just moved here when my mother went to work for your father."

"No, I don't think I've ever heard anyone mention that."

"So we moved here, and she went to work."

"I might as well tell you something else about that. I don't know if it's true or not, but it shadows some of the attitudes in this house."

Marnie looked at him questioningly. "OK," she said hesitantly.

"My mother believes your mother was my father's mistress. Your mother went to work immediately as his executive secretary instead of his promoting someone who already worked at Barrett's and knew about the business. His secretary was getting ready to retire when he went on a business trip. When he came back, your mother moved here and went to work for him. He met her wherever it was he went. My mother thought he met her and brought her here to be his 'piece on the side,' as my mother called it. My parents had an awful fight about it. I can still remember hearing it, even though I must have only been nine or ten. But he wouldn't give in to Mother and fire Pamela—that was your mother's name. He said she was a damn good secretary and he wouldn't tear up his office staff on Mother's say so."

"Do you think she was his mistress?"

"I have no idea. Possibly. But she was an excellent secretary, I know that. He had a hard time replacing her when she died."

"And I went to work there then?"

"You went to work at Barrett's then, and in a way it had to do with her death. Let me start further back in the story, though."

"I'd like to know when and how we met. Your mother made it sound like I was out to catch you from the first."

The smile flickering on his face was not a pleasant one. "She was pretty accurate about that."

Marnie sat back, abashed to think such a thing could be true. At first, she thought maybe Ruth's problem with Pamela had caused her to say the things she had about Marnie, but this statement, at least, was true. She wondered if the other hateful things Ruth said were true.

"To be truthful, we were just kids when we first met. Alice brought you to work with her a couple of times, but being four years younger than I was, and a girl to boot, I didn't pay much attention to you.

"The next time I remember meeting you was when you worked at the Roadhouse. You were in those short shorts and tight tee shirt and flirting with everyone who came in. Everyone in town knew who you were. At least the men did."

Marnie closed her eyes. She screwed up her courage to ask the question she might not like the answer to. "You intimated at lunch that I did more than flirt with the men. Is that so?"

"You gave the impression you slept around, but I don't know if that was true."

She covered her face with her hands. The lavender scent of the hand lotion she had applied earlier soothed her. Breathing deeply, she dropped her hands into her lap.

"Is that when we started dating?"

"No, I was dating Celeste, sort of engaged to be engaged. Our parents were good friends and encouraged the relationship. I used to come to the Roadhouse with my buddies. I'd have a burger and a beer and leave without a female companion. None of our girlfriends would be caught dead in there, but we liked the burgers they served up. I still do. And it was the macho place for guys to go."

"Yes, I thought the burger today was good. I didn't remember the place at all, but I wouldn't have felt terribly out of place eating there as long as you were with me. It was Jolene's outfit and you telling me I dressed the same way that upset me."

David rested his head against the back of the chair and stared up at the ceiling. "Then a couple of years later a tragedy happened."

"Alice told me about the plane crash," Marnie said, softly. "David, I'm so sorry. It must have been terrible for you."

"Yes, it was. Both my father and my Uncle John were killed, and my feelings of loss were not only emotional but also business related. They ran the plant together. The fact that they both died left a very big burden on my shoulders."

"And I was working there by then?"

"Yes, you had gotten fired from the Roadhouse. When your mother died and you had no job, no way to support yourself, my father hired you, out of respect for Pamela, he said. You were kind of frightened then about how you were going to make a living. Your mother had been supporting you after you lost your job, and even though she had a little insurance, you worried about paying the rent. Dad thought highly of your mother so he gave you a job, with the understanding you would have to keep it yourself. That is, you'd have to be on time, show up every day, and do the work assigned to you."

"That's only fair."

"Yes. All that happened a few months after I graduated from college and came back to be trained in the business."

"Is that when we started dating?"

"No." He smiled. "You're still in a hurry, like usual. I'll get to it. Promise."

She smiled back and settled into her chair, trying to be patient and let David tell the story his own way.

"You would flirt with me, all right, any time you saw me. You went wherever the office administrator sent you. As far as I know, you did good work. The only complaint I ever heard was that you flirted with all the men, married or not, and the other women didn't like that. When we met in the hall, you'd say 'Hello, David' in a sexy voice and give me a sizzling look. When we were around other people, you'd call me Mr. Barrett, and your smiles would be slightly less sex-filled. But it was obvious to everyone you were flirting with me."

"How did I dress at work?"

"Your clothes weren't inappropriate, exactly, but you knew just how tight and short and low cut you could get away with. You kept the men in all the offices in a constant state of arousal."

"Did I date any of them?" Marnie asked with a frown. She couldn't wrap her mind around the picture David was painting of her.

"Yes, some of the junior executives."

"Did I—" She tried to build up the courage to ask the question "—did I sleep with them?"

David frowned. "I have no way of knowing for sure, but a couple of them bragged that you did."

She closed her eyes as she felt her cheeks flame in shame.

"They could have been bragging, of course . . . just making it up to seem macho."

"But you believed it?"

"Yes, I believed it. The way you dressed and acted made people believe it could be true."

"Did we date then?"

"Not until after the plane crash. I made it through the funeral without falling apart, but when I was hit with the reality of managing a business that had taken two men with years of experience to run, plus deal with my mother, I couldn't handle it.

"Oh, I went in to work and did what I could, but I couldn't keep my mind on the problems at hand. I started drinking more than I should have. That caused me to spend less time at the plant, less time thinking about how to manage things and more time worrying about failing."

"It was a big burden for anyone, especially for someone so young." Marnie felt empathy for all David had gone through.

"My mother was on the verge of a nervous breakdown. She and my father had just moved into this house, which had been her parents' home before their deaths. All the remodeling she wanted to do came to a stop." He looked around the room. "That's why the largest part of the house looks like this. The last time most of it was redone was fifty years ago.

"Celeste and I were engaged by then. She was angry with me because I couldn't think about the wedding plans. She thought I spent too much time worrying about the business, while I couldn't see how I was going to be able to keep the company afloat with my lack of knowledge. I couldn't be bothered with wedding plans when I had so many other things to think about. I started going to the Roadhouse after work, and that's where I saw you in your short, tight little skirt and low-cut, tight top." He grinned at the memory.

"Was I working there again?"

"No, you just started showing up there in the evenings. You'd go home and change into an even sexier outfit than you had worn to work and go to the Roadhouse. Looking back, I realized Jolene must have called you and let you know when I came in. Or maybe you went there every evening hoping I'd show up. You were just waiting to catch me, but I didn't realize it then. It didn't take you long."

Chapter 16

"You mean I chased you until you caught me?" Marnie said with a grin.

David grinned back. "You could say that, I guess, but it was you who caught me, and good." The smile turned into a frown.

"How?"

"By getting pregnant."

That statement wiped the grin off Marnie's face. She had hoped that part of Ruth's vitriolic tirade had been a lie. From Alice's report earlier, she knew she had been pregnant with Jonathan when they married, but she was still hoping they had married for love. The story David had been telling her was damning, but there was still a chance they had fallen in love during that period, and she had to know which story was true.

"David, I have to know. Were we in love, or did I get pregnant so you would marry me?"

He sighed deeply, leaned back, and closed his eyes. After a few moments he spoke.

"Marnie, I'm trying my best today to set aside any animosity toward you. I'm trying to tell this story as truthfully as I can. With all the shenanigans you have pulled over the last four years, and especially with this last one—and yes, I know I haven't told you yet what it is—I would have said you did it to trap me into marriage. But this last week or so, since you came back as such a different person, when I think back to that period of time, I think maybe we were a little bit in love.

"You see, the Marnie I knew at first had more of the personality I see in you now. You were certainly more of an extrovert, both in your dress and your actions, but more importantly, I could confide in you—share my fears with you." He leaned over and propped his elbows on his knees. "At least after I had a few beers. And you were the only person I could talk to like that."

"Couldn't you talk to Celeste? After all, you were going to be married."

Marnie couldn't believe she had said that to her husband, pointing out the fact he should have been able to talk to his then fiancée.

"Celeste didn't want to talk about anything but wedding plans, and I didn't want to appear weak."

"But you could to me?"

"Yes. That's one thing I've been thinking about this past week. You did listen to me. You soothed and petted me, told me everything was going to be OK. You told me everything I wanted to hear—that I was smart, that I knew more about the business than I thought I did, that I could turn to others for advice on matters I didn't have the know-how on.

"That Marnie, the concerned, kind Marnie, was who I think I fell a little bit in love with." He stood and paced in front of the chairs. "But don't get me wrong, it was the alcohol combined with your seduction that got me into bed with you. Your encouragement worked, however. I turned to some of the top managers in the plant, and with their help, I began to see I could do it."

"So at least I did something right."

He sighed and sat down again. "Yes, I'll admit it. You did something right. But I didn't. I was still engaged to Celeste," he explained, "but I was sleeping with you regularly. I was pretty careless at first when I was drinking so much, but later on I wanted to take precautions against pregnancy. You said you were taking care of it, and I believed you, until the day you came to me and said you were pregnant."

"And so we got married," she said.

"Not at first." David rubbed his eyes. "At first I couldn't believe it. You said you were on the pill. How could you be pregnant? I thought you were just telling me we had a baby on the way to get me to marry you or to get money out of me to stay quiet. By that time I knew how mercenary you were. Money was important to you—very, very important. I had been buying presents to keep you from telling Celeste about our affair. I think you and I would have been over except for the incredible sex we were having. It was like a drug to me. I couldn't leave you alone.

"When you came to me about the pregnancy, though, I was so upset I wouldn't even speak to you. You let me know it was either marriage or you would let the whole town know you were carrying the 'Barrett bastard.' That's what you called him. You deliberately waited to tell me so it was too late to get an abortion."

"An abortion," Marnie said, aghast that she would even consider such a thing.

"Yes, that's what you said. Although I would never have condoned such a thing, no matter what."

"I would hope not. I would certainly hope not!"

"So we drove to Centerview and flew to Las Vegas to get married. It caused some stir when we got back, let me tell you. I had asked you to let me tell Celeste and my mother first, but you went to the Roadhouse and told everyone there, so it spread all over town in a hurry. Both my mother and my fiancée were humiliated."

"Yes, I can see they would be," she replied.

"I had moved back in here with my mother when my father died so she wouldn't be alone. When we married, you moved in, too."

"Had you been living with Celeste?"

"No. She was living with her parents until we married, and I had my own apartment until my father and uncle died.

My mother's life was put on hold. She could barely function, and I thought I needed to live here with her."

Marnie looked around the room. "Well, all this explains the dichotomy in this house."

"Dichotomy?"

"Yes, it means—"

"I know what it means," he interrupted. "I've never heard you use the word before. You always seemed to have a limited vocabulary and would accuse me of putting you down when I used a word you didn't know."

"Really?"

"Really."

She thought for a few seconds and then laughed. "I guess I don't know what words I don't know."

David laughed with her and then grew quiet. "At first we found lots of things we could laugh about together, but by the time Jonathan was born, things had changed."

"Changed how?"

"For one thing, you hated this house. You were always on me about buying a new one, or at least leasing an upscale condo. And Mother was on your case about everything you said and did, which just made you say and do more to upset her."

"Tell me about Mrs. Tucker."

"By the time Jonathan was two weeks old, it was obvious you wouldn't be able to care for him. You didn't want to. His crying upset you—you didn't know what to do about it. Mrs. Tucker had been a nanny for a family Mother knew. Their children had grown, and Mother approached her about caring for Jonathan."

"So she's been with him from the beginning?"

"Just about."

"And she does everything for him? I don't do anything?"

"Your idea of being a good mother is stopping in the nursery on your way out and telling him to be a good boy that day and stopping in the evening to ask how his day had been."

"That's all?" she asked incredulously.

"That's all. Mrs. Tucker has Saturdays and Sundays off. I take him along with me when I can, or one of the maids cares for him if I can't take him to the plant. If I don't have to work, I'll take him to the park or to the movies—something like that."

"Is she good to him, that is, kind?"

"Yes. I wouldn't put up with her if she weren't. But she is so much older she doesn't do as many fun things with him as I would like. She's not exactly cuddly and loving. She's more like a teacher, but she's dependable."

"Why was Celeste caring for him recently?"

"When Mrs. Tucker had to go to her dying sister, Celeste volunteered to come care for him. I think my mother had a hand in that."

"Why?"

"My mother wants me to divorce you and marry Celeste."

"And Celeste is all too ready to step back into your life, right?"

"Right. She got married about six months after we did, but it didn't last long. She's been after me ever since it became obvious our marriage wasn't a happy one."

Marnie looked around the bedroom.

"How long have you been sleeping somewhere else?"

"Ever since I found out about your affair with Ray."

Chapter 17

The room seemed like it was swirling. Marnie gripped the arms of the chair and commanded herself to calm down. Everyone had been giving hints or telling her outright she was cheating on her husband. Now was the time to get it all out in the open.

She took a deep breath. "Who is Ray?"

For a while she thought David was not going to answer her. When he did, his sarcastic voice was back.

"This new you isn't going to deny it?"

"How can I deny it? I don't remember!" her voice rose and cracked. A hint of a sob threatened to take over. *No,* she told herself. *I can't break down again.*

"I don't remember" she repeated more calmly. "Not you and not a bit of what you've told me. Not this Ray. Not even my own son. Now please tell me, who is Ray?"

David's stare threatened her composure. At last he spoke.

"Ray Boling was head of research and development at Barrett's."

"And he and I . . ." She found she couldn't voice it.

"Over the last four years, I suspected you of having affairs several times, but I couldn't prove anything. You always denied it, and since you were still flirting with every man around, it was hard to tell. I thought about hiring a private detective to find out, but I guess I didn't really want to know. Plus, I was so busy getting the plant back to where it was before the deaths of my father and uncle that I let my private concerns slide.

"Then, about six months ago, it became obvious that you and Ray had something going, and when you admitted it, I moved into a guest room. You said you wanted a divorce in order to marry Ray. You made it plain you didn't want 'the kid,' as you called him, but I would have to pay big bucks to get to keep him. 'A judge always gives a kid to his mother,' you said.

"I should have filed for a divorce at that point. Mother and Celeste were trying to get me to do it."

"Why didn't you?"

"I did talk to my lawyer about it, but things were really hectic at the plant, and I kept putting it off. He was drawing up some papers for you to sign to give me custody of Jonathan, but I never seemed to find the time to go by his office to approve and sign them. I would have paid the money you were demanding in order to keep Jonathan.

"At that point, Ray was giving me some funny looks at work, always smirking at me whenever he passed by. I should have known something more was going on than just the affair, as if that wasn't enough."

"Couldn't you have fired him?" Marnie was amazed to find herself on David's side in the matter. "You let him continue to work there?"

"He had a contract, and, unfortunately, sleeping with the boss's wife didn't break any of the terms." He snorted. "I never thought I would need to put not sleeping with my wife as a condition of his employment. Anyway, I was looking into a buyout. That was going to cost big bucks, too, if it could be done. I figured that was what you two were aiming for, lots of money for buying out his contract, lots more for relinquishing your rights to Jonathan, maybe even more just to get a divorce."

"I can't believe this. I just can't believe it," Marnie said as she leaned forward, resting her face in her hands. After a few moments she stood up and started pacing the room, finally stopping and wrapping her arms around the massive bedpost.

"I don't like this person I was—am. I don't like me at all!"

"You weren't very likeable. Sweet and friendly at times, yes. Manipulative, yes. Charming, you bet. But when a person really got to know you, no, you weren't very likeable."

"I can see now why your mother doesn't like me."

"She has lots of reasons not to like you."

"Yes, I agree."

Marnie returned to her chair. "Maybe this is some sort of heavenly retribution, this memory loss. A way to start over."

David gave a snort of disbelief. "You've tried that one too many times for me to believe it again."

"What do you mean?"

"You constantly tell me you're going to be good and not do those things again. You promise. It only lasts until the next time."

"Like what?"

"Staying out until two or three in the morning with no phone call, or even staying out all night. 'I was with the girls,' you would say. And 'I promise I won't do it again.' Until the next time."

Marnie gaped at him, astonished. "I did that?"

"Several times."

She was marveling at her audacity when David spoke again.

"And promising to do something with Jonathan, to take him somewhere, and never showing up."

"Oh, no." She wilted, falling back into the comfort of the chair. "How could I do that to my son?"

"That is why I don't want Jonathan to become close to you and have you disappoint him another time. That's why we have to have Mrs. Tucker, someone who is dependable, care for him," David said angrily. "We sure can't depend on you, and I'm trying to keep his heart from being broken another time." He stood in front of her.

"But I—"

"But you what? Won't do it again? You promise? Your promises aren't worth anything, Marnie. Not anything." He ran his fingers through his hair and walked over to look out the window.

Marnie wanted to say, "I don't remember," but she had uttered those words too many times already. "I thought I wanted to remember my past, but now, after hearing all that, I'd just as soon it never comes back to me."

David turned back to her. "And I'm just waiting until you turn back into the old Marnie. I've come to believe you really do have amnesia. You're not a good enough actress to be putting on this show without losing your temper or giving it away in some manner. But the truth is, when you finally recall your old life, you'll go back to being that way again, and none of us can take that anymore. *I* can't take it anymore."

She sat silently. She reckoned he meant they would be divorced and she would lose Jonathan. That would break her heart, for she had grown to love him in the few short days she had known him. She almost laughed aloud at the thought. She had known him since he was born, but it felt like she had only just met him.

Then another thought occurred, and she raised her eyes to David.

"That first night when I found my way home, Ruth was in the downstairs hall, and she said I wouldn't get away with something. She said I would go to jail. And you have said you need to find something I took. What is that? What else did I do?"

David looked exhausted when he returned to his chair, sinking into it and leaning his head against the back. His eyes looked bleak and sad when he spoke.

"Ray stole the plans and prototype of a secret component the Air Force wants in a newly developed spy drone. He had access to all of it, and he took it. We've spent a lot of time and money in developing the technology. Without it, Barrett's will go under eventually. He was taking it to one of our competitors where he could sell it for millions. Or maybe he was going to sell it to a foreign government. You were, are, with him in the deal."

Chapter 18

"He . . . we . . . stole it?"

"Yes."

"How?"

"Ray put the information—drawings, plans, algorithms, and so forth—on a flash drive, put it in his briefcase along with the prototype of the device, and walked out with it, after destroying the information on the company computer, of course. Then he went to the vault at the bank where we keep offsite backup and took that, too. We would never make it possible for anybody get into the vault alone, but Ray conned another person with clearance into cooperating. We have that person under surveillance. We're trying to decide whether he was a willing accomplice or was duped."

"But . . ." Marnie sputtered, not really understanding what he was telling her. "But what did he do that for? Surely he couldn't do anything with it," she said naively.

"Of course he can. He's going to sell it to a foreign government, or even one of our competitors, who could claim they invented it. It's worth millions."

"Oh my!"

"What's even worse, we had obtained government money to build the thing to this point, plus spent a lot of our own money developing it. If we can't produce something to show them, we'll have to repay the government money, or at least a good portion of it, and that would put Barrett's out of business."

"And that's why you've wanted me to remember what happened?"

"That's it. I've been trying to figure out why you're back here and how come you've lost your memory. When I thought you were just pretending, I figured Ray had sent you back home to act as if you couldn't remember for some reason, maybe to find out what I knew or maybe so I would spend time trying to get information out of you instead of looking for him."

"But you said you don't think I'm acting."

"At first I did, but not anymore. You're too changed. If you remembered, you would have blown your stack by now or reacted in your usual, characteristic ways. You're still you, but calmer, more rational. You seem reasonable, even. And Doctor Means said he was positive you were really ill when you returned."

"What does it all mean, with your prototype and plans still missing and me back?"

"You tell me! You're the one who ran off with Ray!"

"I can't. I can't tell you. I would if I could. You don't realize how awful it is to be clueless about my past. Even worse, everything you are telling me about what kind of person I am is weighing on me like a ton of bricks. On the one hand, I desperately want to remember my past. On the other, I don't want to go back to being the person I was."

"Maybe you and Ray had a falling out over something, if he didn't send you back to delay my search for him, that is. But that doesn't explain your amnesia.

"You were really sick, like Doc said, but not sick enough to affect your memory. And you haven't been in any wreck or been badly injured enough to cause it, either, or else you'd be banged up in some way. So that only leaves a bad emotional trauma, Doctor Means says. But what could that be?"

Marnie got up once again to pace the floor. "No matter what I find out, I've got to know what has happened to me. I can't go through life being this lost person."

"The one thing we haven't talked about is drug use."

"Drug use!" She stopped pacing and stared at her husband. "Don't tell me I used drugs, too!" she said, dreading to hear David's answer.

"No, not to my knowledge. But that doesn't mean you might not have done so after you and Ray left. You might have used something so powerful it knocked you out and left you with no recollection of your past."

"Oh my God! I hope not!" She put her hands over her face. "Please God, don't let that be it!" She dropped her hands. "Couldn't Doctor Means test my blood and find out?"

"I asked him that. He had the sample he took the first night sent here to the local hospital to check for anything relating to your illness, but the local lab can't test for illegal drugs. It would have to be sent off to another lab for that."

"I guess I want to know. I mean, I don't really relish knowing, but I need to know."

"I think it's too late now to do that. It's been too many days. Whatever you took would be out of your system by now."

Marnie resumed her pacing. "Don't you have any idea where we went when we left here?"

"No, I don't know where you went. That's exactly what I want to know. From what I can piece together, you packed a suitcase and met him at Pine Crest Mall. Your car was found in the parking lot. You must have gotten in his car and drove to a small airfield just east of town. He kept a small plane there, and his car was found in the hangar a few days after you two disappeared."

"He was a pilot?"

"Yes. He had mentioned it before, I think, but he didn't talk much about it. After he hatched this plan, I don't think he wanted people remembering that he could fly. Anyway, he had kept a plane out there for several months—rented a hangar to keep it in out of the weather and away from anyone spotting it and connecting it to him. The man who rented out the space called the plant looking for him a week or so after you and he went missing. Seems Ray owed rent on the hangar, and the owner wanted paid. Ray's car was inside where the plane had been. So he flew out of here, that much is certain, but where he went I don't know. We assumed you were with him, but we didn't know for sure. As far as we knew, he could have killed you to keep you from telling the authorities anything about his plans."

"Didn't he have to file a flight plan or something?"

"At a small field like that, the pilot doesn't have to file anything. Mostly agricultural flights, what they used to call crop dusters, fly out of there, and local pilots who take a plane up on a pretty afternoon for the fun of it. Folks who fly to neighboring towns for the high school football and basketball games keep planes out there, or rent one from the man who owns the place. That's about all.

"Where you went, I don't know. Why you're back, I don't know. How you got back, I don't know."

"And what happened to me to cause me to lose my memory neither one of us knows."

Chapter 19

When Marnie woke up the next morning, she felt as if some of her burden had been lifted.

How odd that I feel better, she thought, *since I found out so much bad stuff about myself yesterday.*

At least it was out in the open—those reasons why everyone thought the worst about her. She was sure she hadn't heard about all the bad things she had done, but she got the general idea. And although anybody else would have been depressed upon hearing all David had told her, in a way she was relieved that her past was no longer a secret. She hoped there was nothing else to surprise her and that she had heard the worst. She would hold on to that thought, anyway, unless told differently.

She had spent the last week getting well, worrying about who she was and what she had done. Now it was time to move on with her life, as best she could.

David had told her, when she asked, that she did not work anywhere, nor did she do any volunteer work. As far as he could tell, he said, she shopped and visited with friends during the day and went out with friends in the evenings. She had no hobbies he knew of.

As she dressed in jeans and a red sweater she thought about what David said about her scant amount of time with Jonathan.

I'm going to change that pattern, she thought. *I'm going to spend more time with him, do things with him, get to really know him—what he likes and doesn't like. A mother needs to know all that.*

Although her husband had cautioned her about disappointing Jonathan again, she was sure she wouldn't go back to ignoring him as she had in the past. She stopped at the nursery and found Mrs. Tucker and Jonathan getting ready for breakfast.

"I was just coming to see if I could join you, or you join me, for breakfast. May I?"

"Sure!" Jonathan said excitedly. "We were just going down to the kitchen to eat."

"Certainly, Mrs. Barrett. Of course you may join us," the older woman said. She appeared to be flustered, wringing a handkerchief in her hands and taking a few steps to and fro. Every few seconds her slender fingers would dart to her cheek. Marnie surmised this was something out of the ordinary, breakfasting with her son, and it made Mrs. Tucker nervous.

"I don't know what the custom is for breakfast—that is, I've forgotten. I've been getting my breakfast delivered on a tray, but now that I'm back on my feet I can go to breakfast instead of breakfast coming to me," she said, smiling at Jonathan, who gave a giggle at the lame joke.

"We usually have our meal in the kitchen," Mrs. Tucker said. "The elder Mrs. Barrett eats in her room, and Mr. Barrett's schedule varies. Sometimes he eats with us. Other times he has already left for work by the time we go downstairs."

The trio descended the staircase and passed through the dining room and into the large kitchen. There were two places set at the island, where brightly striped pottery plates were set on cheerful yellow placemats.

"Here now, Mrs. Gravy has to put out another place at the table," the cook said in a jolly voice. "We have a new one this morning, we do." She winked at Jonathan. "Yer mother's joining us today, is she?"

"Yes, ma'am," he replied, politely.

"Well, it's oatmeal this morning. Will that be suitin' ye this mornin', Miss Marnie?"

"Yes indeed. As far as I know, I like oatmeal."

The rotund cook placed bowls of steaming oatmeal in front of each person and started pouring orange juice into their glasses when the swinging door opened and David joined the group.

"Ah, now we have everyone here, we do. Oatmeal this mornin', Mr. David?"

David lifted his eyebrows as he observed the three people at the breakfast bar.

"Er, OK, Mrs. Gravy, uh, Grady."

Marnie was looking into her oats as she stirred them. "Mrs. Grady, would you happen to have any brown sugar handy? And some butter? I think I'd like some on my oatmeal."

"Lord love ye', o' course I do. Not that you've been eatin' breakfast much lately, but I remember what people like, I do, and I have it all ready for ye'." She reached over to the counter and put two small covered bowls in front of Marnie.

"There ye' go. Had the butter out softenin' and here's yer brown sugar, just like you like it," she said as she pushed the bowls forward.

"That's what you like on your oats?" Jonathan asked.

"I think so. That's what my appetite is telling me. Isn't it funny I can't remember much, but I know what I like on oatmeal?" She smiled at her son.

"I like raisins in mine," he said, reaching for the bowl sitting in front of his place.

"And here's some sausage that goes well with it," Mrs. Grady said as she put a plate of links in front of David, who immediately forked several onto his plate.

"Mrs. Gravy knows what I like, too," he said.

Mrs. Tucker had taken a few spoons of the porridge when she pushed it away. "Mr. Barrett, I hate to ask, I really do, but could someone watch Jonathan for a while this morning? I have a toothache. It's very bad or else I would put it off until my day off, but I really need to see my dentist about it. I have been taking more pain reliever than is safe. I wouldn't ask if it wasn't necessary."

Marnie spoke up immediately, before David had a chance to answer.

"I was going to ask him to spend the morning with me anyway, to show me around the house, and perhaps help me remember things. And I thought we could read or watch a movie on TV."

David looked from one woman to the other. "Mrs. Tucker, of course you can take as much time as is necessary. Marnie, are you sure you're up to caring for Jonathan for several hours?"

"I'm sure," she answered as she looked at him expectantly.

"OK then. Mrs. Tucker, do you need me to drive you to the dentist's office?"

"No, thank you, Mr. Barrett. I can make it. I'll leave right now." She placed her napkin neatly by her plate and left the room.

"Poor woman," Mrs. Grady said as she gathered the uneaten breakfast and carried the dishes to the sink. "A sore tooth can give a body a right lot of trouble, all right."

"I noticed her touching her cheek when I stopped in the nursery this morning, but I thought it was nerves."

"And you're sure you're OK caring for Jonathan for the morning?"

"Of course! Why wouldn't I be?"

"It's just that you've never done it before. You've said he—that it made you uneasy to be in charge of a child."

"Nonsense! We'll do just fine. Won't we, Jonathan?"

Jonathan nodded, his mouth too full to speak, but his eyes were bright as he looked at her.

"Well, if you have any problems, Alice will be to work before long, and Mrs. Grady is here. You can leave him with either of them if you need to." He had finished his meal and pushed back his stool. "Good breakfast, Mrs. Grady," he said, and after giving Jonathan a kiss on the top of his head, he left the room.

"If you're through eating, Jonathan, let's go get washed up before we start our morning activities."

I must really have been pathetic if David thinks I can't even care for my son for a few hours. I'll show him. I may have been a bad mother before, but I'm going to learn to be a good mother to my son from this day forward.

Chapter 20

Jonathan's schedule included brushing his teeth after meals, so each of them went to their own room to complete their preparations for the day, meeting in the hall a few minutes later.

"Jonathan, maybe you can help me remember things around here."

"OK," he said. "How?"

"Let's start by you telling me about all these rooms up here. There are a lot of them, and I don't know who they belong to. That is, I don't know who sleeps in them. Are they all bedrooms?" She hadn't wanted to open any of the doors for fear of prying or invading someone's privacy. "Will you be a tour guide and tell me about this house?"

"Sure." He took her by the hand and pulled her back to stand in front of her own room. Pointing across the hall, he started his explanation.

"That's Mrs. Tucker's room," he said, "right across from yours."

"Yes, and the next one is yours."

He opened the door to his room and led her inside. "See, there's a door from my room to hers, so if I get scared during the night I can just go get her, or I can yell and she will come."

"Do you get scared often?"

"No. I used to when I was little, but now that I'm four I never do."

"That's good."

"That door"—he pointed to a door in his bedroom opposite the one to Mrs. Tucker's room—"goes to the play room."

"Yes. We came through it the other day when you were showing me around."

They went into the room where she usually spent time with Jonathan.

"Do you spend a lot of time here? Or do you go other places?"

"I spend *lots* of time here," he said dramatically. "We almost *never* go anyplace else."

"Really? Do you ever go to the park, or to a friend's house, or any place like that?"

"When it's warm, we sometimes go to the park. Daddy says it will be spring soon and maybe Mrs. Tucker will take me to the park with the swings and slides and things. We used to go there before it was winter."

"That sounds like fun."

"It is. I like the slide and the teeter-totter. But I can't play on the teeter-totter unless there's someone about my size to do it with. Mrs. Tucker doesn't like to push it up and down for me. She says it hurts her back. But Daddy does it when he takes me."

"Don't you have any friends about your age you can go with?"

He looked sad. "No. I don't have any friends."

"Do you ever go to a school, like pre-school?"

"No. Mrs. Tucker teaches me my numbers and ABCs. Grandmother says we pay her to do that and Daddy shouldn't pay someone else to do the same thing."

Well, Marnie thought, *there's more to pre-school than just learning the alphabet and numbers. There's making friends and playing games and learning to work in a group. I'll have to see about that.*

"So what about the rest of the rooms on this floor?" she asked, leading the boy back out into the hall.

"Daddy sleeps in that one," he said, pointing to the last room at the opposite end of the hall from hers.

As far away from me as he can get, she thought.

"How about the rest of them?"

"Nobody sleeps in them. They used to, a long time ago, but they don't live here anymore. Now they're for company, but we don't ever have any company."

"Let's go downstairs, and you can tell me about the rooms down there."

"OK," he said and led the way down.

They went into the living room first. It was as dreary and gloomy as it had appeared the first time she had seen it.

"This is the living room," Jonathan said. "I'm not allowed to play here. I can't be in here unless an adult is with me."

"Well, I'm an adult and I'm with you, so you can be here."

He grinned at her. "Yep." He quickly looked solemn. "I mean yes."

"Are you not allowed to say 'yep'?"

"The kids at the playground say it all the time, but Mrs. Tucker and Grandmother say I should talk properly at all times."

"Hmm." Marnie would not allow herself to say anything else about the subject. "I didn't notice those portraits over the fireplace when I was in here before."

"That's Grandfather and his brother, Uncle John."

"I see."

"They died before I was borned."

"Born. They died before you were born."

"Yes, before I was born." He struggled to not put the final -ed on the word, and Marnie smiled at his efforts.

"This doesn't seem like a room I want to spend much time in. Let's go on, shall we?"

The next room on their tour was the library.

"I came in here the other day," Marnie told him. "There are a lot of books, but I don't think I saw any for children."

"Daddy uses this for an office sometimes when he works at home. That's the only time I can come in here. He gives me paper to draw on while he works. I don't think there are any kid books in here."

"That portrait, is it your grandfather?"

"Yes. It's Daddy's father. Daddy says that makes him my grandfather," he said, looking at Marnie to see if she followed.

"Yes, that's right."

The next two doors down the hall were ones she had not opened the first time she ventured into this part of the house. Jonathan put his hand on the first door they came to as he spoke. "This is a great big closet with a lot of old stuff in it." He advanced to the next door and opened it. "Alice said they call this the ladies' card room 'cause folks used to play cards in it a long time ago, when my grandfather lived here."

"Let's see the next room," Marnie suggested.

They entered the sunny room at the end of the hall.

"Sometimes Mrs. Tucker likes to sit here. I bring my cars and play on the floor while she reads."

"It's a very nice room. I like it a lot."

"Me, too."

Marnie thought the side yard that was visible from the sunroom would be an ideal place for a swing set and other outside toys for Jonathan to enjoy. She wondered if he had a set somewhere.

"Jonathan, do you have a swing set or climbing set or anything like that in the yard?"

He looked sad when he answered. "No. I have to get Daddy or Mrs. Tucker to take me to the park to play on stuff like that."

She wondered if she could convince David to have some play equipment installed in the yard come spring—if she was still there by then. She couldn't imagine David tolerating a wife who had done all he told her she had done.

The next room on the tour was on the right as they left the sunroom. Jonathan told her matter-of-factly, "This is the men's card room."

In it was not only a poker table, but a pool table as well, with all the trappings that accompanied it. Balls were scattered around the massive table, and a rack on the wall held pool cues.

"Does your daddy teach you how to play pool?"

"No. He said he will when I get older."

The next room on that side of the hall was the room she had previously discovered. Bright and sunny, it was welcoming to the pair.

"I think I like this room best," she told Jonathan.

"I like it, too," he agreed. "I like my room and the playroom and this room bestest of all."

"What do they call it?"

"The TV room."

"Do you come here and watch TV?"

"Sometimes Daddy and I do, when it's raining and we can't go outside to play. We come in here and watch a movie."

Marnie sat in one of the overstuffed chairs that were scattered around the room and patted the one beside her. "Come sit here so we can talk."

Jonathan did as he was told, sliding back to snuggle into the pillows lining the chair.

"Remember when I said you could help me remember?"

He nodded his head enthusiastically.

"I want you to try to remember any time you saw me in any of these rooms we've talked about this morning. Remember who was there with me and what was going on, what I said, and what the other people said to me. OK?"

Chapter 21

Jonathan's forehead wrinkled, and he studied his hands, which were clasped together in his lap. He seemed to be in deep thought.

"When we were in the living room, I told you who those men in the pictures were."

"Yes, sweetie, I know. That was this morning, just a while ago. Can you think of another time I was in any of these rooms? Before I went away, I mean."

Jonathan twisted his hands together tightly. It seemed to Marnie as though her question had upset him. She thought there must have been some incident that had happened earlier, something he didn't want to tell her about. Whatever it was, she didn't want to distress him. She wouldn't force him to remember something he'd rather forget.

"That's OK if you don't."

"I don't," he said, a relieved expression spreading over his face. "I don't remember ever being in any of the rooms with you before. Just yesterday and today."

"OK. Let's forget it. We'll start all over again from when I came back, and you can forget anything that happened before then. OK?"

He nodded.

"Are there any games or puzzles in this room that are yours?"

He slid from the chair and ran over to a cabinet. He threw open the doors and started to search through the boxes.

I must have really been some kind of a pathetic mother if my son doesn't even want to talk about what went on before,

Marnie thought. *I've forgotten it, and he obviously wants to. So we'll just put the past in the past and start over.*

"Here's a puzzle Daddy and I like to work together," Jonathan said, pulling a colorful box from the stack.

"Would you like to work it with me?" Marnie asked.

"Yes. We work puzzles on this table," he said, as he opened the box and dumped the pieces on the table in front of the window and spread them out. "First you turn all the pieces right side up," he said, demonstrating. "And then you find the edges. See?" he said, holding up a piece to show Marnie. "See how it's straight on one side?"

"Yes, I see that. I can see you really know how to do this. You must be a very good puzzle worker."

"I am. Daddy says so," he answered proudly.

While they were working the puzzle, Mrs. Tucker came to the door. "I'm back from the dentist, Mrs. Barrett. I can take Jonathan upstairs now, if you wish."

Marnie noticed the crestfallen look that spread across Jonathan's face.

"I'd just as soon keep him with me, Mrs. Tucker. He's great company. You go on and rest. Take a nap if you want. Jonathan and I are doing just fine."

Jonathan's face beamed with that, and when Mrs. Tucker left, they went back to their project.

When the picture of marine animals and ocean waves was assembled, admired, and taken apart again, Marnie asked, "So, what should we do next?"

"I like games."

"Then let's play a game. What do you have?"

Jonathan proceeded to find a game and instruct her in the rules. After half an hour of winning and losing game pieces, she asked, "Do you have any more games?"

"No, I don't think so," he answered.

How sad, she thought. *How many games there must be for children his age, and he only has one. Doesn't anyone ever buy him anything?* Then the truth hit her; she was the one who should have been buying them. *I'm going to have to do something about this. If I'm going to be a good mother, I need to get him things he needs. There is obviously no shortage of money in this house. I'll have to talk to David about buying some things for my son.*

"Are there any playing cards here?"

"Sure," he said as he pulled open a drawer in the table and produced a deck.

"Do you ever play Go Fish?"

Jonathan looked puzzled. "Gold Fish?"

"No, Go Fish."

Marnie explained the game as he sat in rapt attention.

After playing for some time, Jonathan once again pronounced the dreaded "Go Fish," and Marnie moaned in exaggerated despair. As he cackled delightedly, a voice sounded from the doorway.

"It sounds like someone's having fun in here!"

"Daddy!" Jonathan rushed to hug his father around the knees. "We're playing Go Fish!"

"So I heard."

"I learned how. And I got threes. And she needed sevens. And I didn't have any, and I told her to Go Fish!" he related animatedly.

"This game is a lot more fun with three people instead of two," Marnie said.

"Please, Daddy, please play with us."

"Well, just for a little bit. I just came home to see how you were doing," David said, looking directly at Marnie.

"We're doing fine. We've worked a puzzle and played a game with cherries and buckets, which he says is the only game he has, and now we're playing Go Fish," she said, smiling broadly at David.

After two rousing rounds of Jonathan's now-favorite game, David called a halt.

"I think it's time for lunch. I'll join you and then I have to get back to work."

Jonathan gathered the cards and put them back into the drawer.

As they walked down the hall, David told Jonathan, "You better wash up before going to the kitchen. We'll meet you there."

"OK," Jonathan replied and opened the last door on the right which was obviously a powder room.

"I think I'd better wash my hands, too," Marnie said.

"There's another powder room off the east hall, too," David replied as they walked through the living room.

"Will Ruth be joining us for lunch?"

"No. Mother eats breakfast and lunch in her suite of rooms. It's like a separate apartment for her. She does like to have dinner here," he said as they passed through the dining room. "I think you are recovered enough to join us tonight."

"All right. What time?"

"Six o'clock. Be on time." He glanced at her attire. "Mother is old school. You'd better dress more formally than jeans. Wear a dress."

Chapter 22

"What do you wear to dinner with someone who hates you?" Marnie mused aloud as she looked through her closet. With as many choices as she had, she was having trouble coming up with something appropriate. She had tried on several dresses, but when she looked in the cheval mirror, she realized each was too short, too tight, or showed too much cleavage for a family dinner.

Where in the world did I wear all these things? she wondered again.

Finally, she came upon a pink knit dress with long sleeves and a high, rounded neckline. The hemline reached mid-calf, and when she tried it on, it fit perfectly. She added high-heeled black boots and admired the look.

It needs a piece of jewelry, she reflected. Rummaging through the drawers in the dressing room didn't produce anything suitable and then she remembered seeing something in the drawer of the dresser in the bedroom. Among the bits and pieces, she found a small, ornately jeweled pin. Only costume jewelry, she was sure, but it was a nice brooch from years gone by, a circle of silver swirls and leaves, set with pink, ruby, and clear stones.

Satisfied at last with her outfit, she added a touch of lipstick and went downstairs. The big grandfather clock standing in the foyer was chiming six when she reached the last step. David was pulling out a chair for his mother as she entered the dining room.

"Good evening," she greeted them.

"Good evening," David said as he rounded the table. She thought his eyes lit up at the sight of her. "You look lovely tonight."

"Thank you."

"Good evening, Ruth." She was determined to be pleasant to her mother-in-law, though she was in agreement that Ruth had every right to be angry with her.

The older woman remained silent.

"Mother, let's do our best to get along tonight."

"I don't know why you are bending over backwards to be nice to a woman who cuckolded you and stole from you—from us. What she did endangers not only your future, but your son's and mine as well. She ought to be in jail like the criminal she is, not sitting down to dinner with us."

"I asked Marnie to join us for dinner tonight. She's not going to remember anything sitting in her room alone for meals. I'm hopeful that something we say, some conversation, will trigger her memory, bring back what she's lost."

"And you believe this—this ridiculous story of hers? You believe she can't remember anything before the day she came stumbling back here?"

"Yes, I do believe it, and so does Doctor Means. If you were around her for long and were open-minded enough, you'd believe it, too. She simply doesn't behave like she used to."

At that moment Mrs. Grady came through the swinging door from the kitchen bearing a platter, which she sat at the end of the large table where David, Ruth, and Marnie were seated.

"A glorious roast, if I do say so meself. 'Twere a good cut and roasted up nicely, it did."

With this pronouncement she left the dining room and returned with a bowl of potatoes and carrots, Mary following along with fragrant rolls and a bowl of salad.

Marnie spread her napkin in her lap.

"This looks absolutely delicious, Mrs. Grady. I didn't think I was hungry until I smelled your cooking."

"Well, now. Everyone enjoy. Is there anything else you need before I leave for the night?"

"No, nothing, Mrs. Grady," Ruth said. "Mary can take care of our needs."

"There's raspberry mousse for dessert," she said as she turned toward the kitchen. "Mary will fetch it when you're ready."

"You're lucky to have such an excellent cook," Marnie said.

"She's too familiar," Ruth grumbled. "When I have a formal affair, I have to tell her to stay in the kitchen. She would be chatting with the guests if I didn't put my foot down."

"She's been here since I was young," David said. "She's like one of the family."

Ruth sniffed at that statement.

"Everything I've eaten has been delicious: blueberry muffins, soup, this roast, and all the meals she sent up to me. Every meal is perfect." She was wondering how many hours the older woman worked every day, but she didn't think she could ask such a thing. David spoke up, though, and seemed to read her thoughts.

"Mrs. Grady lives over what we call the carriage house in the back of this house. She has a nice apartment there. She says she likes just walking across the yard and not having to worry about getting to and from work. She fixes breakfast for everyone, and sometimes she fixes lunch. It depends on whether anyone is going to be home or not. If it's just Jonathan and Mrs. Tucker, she may leave soup or simple leftovers for them to warm up. Most afternoons Mrs. Grady goes to her apartment and takes a nap then returns to finish preparing dinner. She has Saturday and Sunday off, and we eat what there is or go out. Mother likes to eat at the country club with her friends."

"It sounds like that works out well for everyone," Marnie agreed.

Ruth ate silently, not adding anything further to the conversation.

"I see you found your mother's brooch," David commented, looking at the ornament pinned to her dress.

Marnie's hand went to the silver circle, and her fingers traced the leaves. "My mother's? This was my mother's?"

Ruth paused her eating, her hand frozen in place. She looked as if the bite of food she had just taken was rotten. As she stared at the jeweled adornment, her mouth twisted into a sneer.

"Yes," David answered. "She wore it to work often. I complimented her on it once, and she told me it was precious to her. She said it had been her mother's," he said, glancing at his mother.

"I found it in a drawer. I had no idea."

Ruth took the napkin from her lap and placed it beside her plate.

"I can't eat any more. I'm going to my room," she pronounced, and before David could get up and help her with her chair, she had risen and marched from the room.

Marnie looked helplessly at David.

"It wasn't anything you said or did"—he laid his hand atop hers and squeezed it—"I shouldn't have brought up your mother. I told you she was sensitive about Pamela."

He withdrew his hand and started eating again. "I appreciate your dressing appropriately and being on time tonight."

"I take it that is something unusual for me, since you're mentioning it?"

"You might say that. It was hard for you to be anywhere on time, and it drives my mother crazy for people to be late for anything, especially dinner. I sometimes think you do it just to aggravate her. And when she complains about the way you dress, you'll wear an even more provocative outfit the next time."

Marnie didn't know what to say about the actions she couldn't remember.

"I have something to confess," David said, glancing up at her.

"Something to confess?"

"Yes. This was a test, of sorts. I wanted to see if you would be late, as usual, and what you would choose to wear."

"I see. Well, it almost got me. I was almost late because I had to try on so many dresses to find one that wasn't too short or too low cut, much less too tight."

He laughed. "I imagine that's right."

Mary entered the room from the kitchen. "Is there anything you need, Mr. David?"

"We're ready for dessert now, Mary." He turned to Marnie. "Am I rushing you?"

"No. If I don't stop now I won't have room for raspberry mousse. It sounds delicious. And"—she laughed—"all my dresses will be too tight for sure."

David laughed with her. "Well, you've never shied away from shopping for new dresses."

Suddenly, she became serious. "David, that's something I need to talk to you about."

"Shopping?" he asked.

He thinks I want to shop for myself, she thought.

"Yes, for Jonathan. He doesn't seem to have many games and puzzles. The books he has look well worn. Does Mrs. Tucker shop for him? Or do you?"

David's face cleared and then a sheepish look came over him.

"To tell the truth, I am the one who is supposed to. Mrs. Tucker can barely be persuaded to buy clothing for him. I've been so busy at work I haven't lived up to my obligations in that regard. What with your disappearance and all the trouble surrounding it, I haven't thought about shopping for Jonathan. Mrs. Tucker told me several weeks ago he was outgrowing his clothes."

"Yes, I noticed how short his pants are. They grow fast at that age."

"How do you know?"

She shot him a puzzled look. "I don't know how I know. Do I know anyone who has a child his age?" She dropped her head, shamefaced. "Anyone besides me—us, I mean?"

"Not that I know of. Maybe one of your friends from the Roadhouse?"

"I can't remember, David. I just can't remember. I just know little children grow fast."

"I'll have to do something about it," he said. "I'll have to take some time and do it."

"I'd like to do it, if you'll let me, but I don't know how to manage it."

"What do you mean?"

"I mean do I drive? Do I have a car? Where do I go to shop? What do I use for money?"

"Oh, all that."

"Yes, all that."

"I hadn't thought about it, but now that you mention it, since you came back without your wallet, you don't have any of your usual necessities. I'll tell you what. I'll go tomorrow and see about getting you a new driver's license. I'll give you some money and a credit card. But"—he paused and looked sternly at her—"it will have a limit on it."

"Fair enough."

"You have a car in the garage." He took her left hand in his. "But you are missing something far more important than your driver's license and credit cards."

"What? What else am I missing?"

Instead of squeezing her hand as he had before, he turned it and traced her ring finger from the tip to the base. "Where, my dear, is your wedding ring and the three carat so-called engagement ring you insisted I buy you after we eloped?"

Chapter 23

Marnie rubbed the spot on her left ring finger. *How could I have overlooked a missing wedding ring? I guess I forgot about it the same way I forgot about my marriage, my son, and my entire life,* she thought. *An engagement ring that size must be worth a lot of money. Did I sell it? Give it to my lover?*

She sighed. She was so tired of being confronted with yet another situation that revealed what an appalling person she was. Yet David had not accused her of anything, only asked if she remembered what had happened to the rings

Marnie clung to the hope that when she did recall what had happened to her there would be a legitimate reason she had acted the way she did—a reason that made sense to her. Until then, she was going to have to do the best she could to regain her life and make amends to her son and husband.

She tossed and turned during the night, unable to fall asleep because of all the things swirling around in her head. As a result, she slept late, and Jonathan and Mrs. Tucker had already eaten breakfast and returned to the nursery when Marnie stopped in. When she entered the room, Jonathan was busy telling Mrs. Tucker the sounds the various letters made and sounding out words.

Jonathan surprised her by rushing to hug her around the knees as he had done to his father the day before. It was the first time her son had hugged her or shown any affection toward her, and as she bent to put her arms around him, tears threatened to spill from her eyes.

After hearing him read several words and praising his progress, Marnie excused herself.

"I'd better go eat some breakfast myself. I'll see you later in the day," she said. "You can finish your lessons while I'm gone."

When she entered the kitchen, she found Mrs. Grady sitting at the granite island looking through a notebook. "Good mornin', luv," she said. "You slept in, I see. What can I fix you for breakfast? Some nice eggs?"

"No, don't get up, Mrs. Grady. I just want some toast and juice, and I can get it myself."

"Then I'll let you. I'm trying to come up with something to cook for supper—er, dinner, Mrs. Ruth calls it—something we haven't had a hundred times before. What do you fancy?"

"I don't know," Marnie answered as she poured her orange juice. She retrieved her toast and sat across from the cook at the wide bar. "Chicken, maybe? I think I like chicken."

"Chicken, you say? Yes, that does sound just right for today. Maybe a nice fricassee."

As Marnie was eating her second piece of toast, David's head and shoulders peaked through the swinging door.

"Ah, there you are. When you're through eating, Marnie, come down to the library, please." With no more than that, he withdrew, leaving the door swinging in his wake.

What did I do now? Every day it seems like I find out another of my misdeeds.

When she entered the library a few minutes later, she found David sitting behind the massive desk, making notes and putting papers into a folder.

"I've been getting you squared away this morning." He shoved a card across the desk. "Here's a new driver's license. I went to the courthouse and told them you had lost yours and needed a new one. Since everything was on the computer, it was easy enough for them to pull up your record and print a new card for you. Of course, it has a different number than the old one. If anyone tries to use the old one, it will alert authorities immediately."

Marnie felt awkward standing in front of the desk like a wayward school child in front of the principal, so she sat down in one of the chairs facing the desk. David pushed another card toward her.

"Here's a credit card in your name. Since the bill comes to me, I'll know where you charge things, Marnie, and how much. It has a limit on it, so you can't go wild buying things."

"I wasn't going to go wild," she told him stiffly. "I was only going to buy Jonathan some things, some toys and books."

He ignored her comment and continued, "I canceled your old credit cards after you and Ray had been gone a few days. I left them active for that long on the recommendation of the detective I hired to find you."

"You hired someone to find me? It sounds like you thought you were better off without me."

"Maybe. But I wanted my project back. It's worth a lot more than you were," he answered sarcastically.

She remained silent, absorbing that statement as he continued.

"You two were smart enough to know I could find out where you were if you used your credit card. Ray had closed out his bank account before you took off, so I assume you were using his cash so you wouldn't leave a paper trail."

He reached into his back pocket and took out his wallet. Taking several bills from it, he tossed them onto the desk. "Here's some cash, too. Take care how you spend it. I'm not going to be as generous as I have been in the past. Or maybe I should say I'm not going to be the pushover I once was."

"Thank you, David. It really is kind of you to do this, since evidently I've been a poor wife and mother. I promise you I won't spend any on myself. This is for Jonathan."

"And finally," he said, pushing a cell phone toward her, "here's a new cell phone. I've programmed three numbers into it: my cell phone, my office phone, and the house phone."

She picked it up and flipped it open.

"If you call the office number, you'll get my secretary, Virginia. She knows your voice, and she knows about your amnesia. If you need me when I'm at work, it's probably best if you call me through that number. That way you won't interrupt a meeting or another phone call."

"Thank you," she said. These few things gave her the feeling she was getting back to a normal life, although she still had no idea what a normal life for her felt like.

He stood up behind the desk. "Go get a coat on. I want to see if you remember how to drive before I give you the keys to your car."

A few minutes later they slid into the seats of the red Mustang. She adjusted the driver's seat forward a bit and moved the rearview mirror so she could use it.

"We messed up your seating when we retrieved it from the mall parking lot," David explained.

She started the engine, backed out, and drove around the house toward the street.

"Take a right. You'll always take a right coming out of the drive to go anywhere in town," he instructed.

He directed her through town, at first taking the same route they had driven to the Roadhouse, then branching off on a different street. After a couple of miles, they came to an intersection adjacent to an interstate highway.

"There's the mall on your right. Pull in there."

Marnie did as he said and drove about halfway along the expanse of the large building. She pulled into a parking place but didn't turn off the motor.

"I think I can find this place again," she said. "It's easy enough to get here."

David was looking out the car window, looking grim but saying nothing.

"What's the matter? Did I do something wrong?"

"You just happened to park in the same spot you used when you abandoned the car and left with Ray. Coming back to the scene of your crime, perhaps?"

"Oh, David . . ."

"Don't say it! Don't say 'I don't remember' one more time. I'm sick and tired of hearing it!"

"Well I'm sick and tired of saying it!" she lashed out.

Frustrated, she closed her eyes and held her mouth tightly closed to avoid saying something she would be sorry for. At last she opened them and said, "Thank you, David. You're being very generous considering my past behavior."

"I want you to know I am only doing this in order to give you enough rope to hang yourself. That is, enough freedom to lead me to Ray and my stolen property. I have no doubt you will. You will begin to remember, and when that happens, you'll be in touch with Ray, wherever he is.

"And there is one more thing, Marnie, one restriction. You are not, under any circumstance, to take Jonathan away from the house. I will not give you the chance to run away with him. You can leave, but not with my son."

Chapter 24

When Marnie had calmed down enough to think about it, she realized David was right, but the prohibition against taking Jonathan shopping stung like a hot iron. If she were in David's shoes, she wouldn't have trusted her either. She might have taken Jonathan and demanded money to return him, or even worse, reverted to being a negligent mother.

She would have liked to take Jonathan shopping, let him help pick out his own toys and clothes, but she would just have to do the best she could to make choices she thought he would like. Maybe one day she could regain David's trust. *Or gain it in the first place*, she thought.

David remained quiet on the way home. Marnie figured the coincidence that she had picked the same parking spot where she had earlier abandoned her car had thrown him into his sullen contemplation. She almost hated to ask anything of him, considering his tone when he last spoke to her, but she steeled her nerve and voiced her request.

"Would you mind showing me where the library is located? I thought I might like to check out some books for Jonathan."

For a minute she thought he wasn't going to answer her, but then he told her to take the next street to the right and pointed out a large red brick structure a block off the main street.

"I doubt you have a library card," he said sarcastically.

"I'll get one," came her curt answer.

She was growing weary of being on the defensive all the time. She knew she had done some unforgiveable things, and she was well aware of the fact that David was tired of hearing her say she didn't remember. But she was equally tired of saying it. What happened was in the past. She had to move on.

"I'll get a damned library card. I'll buy Jonathan the things he needs. I will not kidnap him. And I will not apologize any more for things I do *not* remember doing!"

When they reached home, she left the car in the circle drive and slammed the driver's door as she exited the vehicle. Storming up the front steps, her escape came to an abrupt halt when she tried to open the massive front door and found it locked.

David was smirking when he came up behind her.

"I was wondering when the old Marnie would come back," he said, using his key to unlock the door. "And here she is."

Holding back on any retort, Marnie ran up the stairs to take refuge in her bedroom. She threw herself onto her bed and pounded her fists into a soft pillow.

"Now that the old Marnie is back, are you ready to tell me where Ray is? Where are the prototype and plans?" David's voice asked from the doorway.

She sat up and threw the pillow at him. It fell to the floor far short of the intended target.

"I've told you and told you. *I don't remember!* I don't remember anything before waking up in that park. Asking me over and over isn't going to help me remember. And I apologize for any and all the bad things I've ever done to you! I apologize for tricking you into marriage! I apologize for not being a good wife, a faithful wife! I apologize for not being a good mother to Jonathan!" She climbed off the bed and came to stand before him. "And I'll tell you one more thing. I'm tired of saying 'I don't remember,' and I'm tired of apologizing. This is the last time I'll do it.

"You can take it or leave it. Believe me or not. There is nothing more I can do or say to change your mind about me. I've got to start living this life. What's that cliché, 'This is the first day of the rest of your life'? Well, it is. I've got to start living my life from this day forward."

David crossed his arms and leaned against the doorframe, a grin playing around his mouth.

Marnie continued. "I think it's time you decided what you want from this point. Do you want a divorce? Are you going to put me out of the house? Just stop asking me things I don't remember. If anything, anything at all, comes back to me, I'll tell you. I promise. But stop badgering me."

She turned and walked away from him.

"I've got to start figuring out what I'm going to do. If I knew what skills I had, I could look for a job. And don't you dare"—she turned suddenly and pointed a finger at him— "don't you dare suggest I go back to work at the Roadhouse! I'm not working in a place like that!"

She walked to the window and looked out. "Alice told me I went to business school and worked in an office for a while. Maybe I have computer training or typing or something." She turned toward him again.

"But if you're going to divorce me, tell me. I've got to start figuring out how to support myself."

He quietly observed her. Finally he spoke.

"That's certainly what I had in mind when you left. Without a doubt you didn't want to be married to me, since you ran off with your lover. I don't see how either of us can expect this marriage to survive. There is nothing left of what wasn't much of a marriage to begin with, but I'm not ready to divorce you right now. As long as I have you here, it won't be long until Ray comes sniffing around again, if only to find out what's going on. If you had a fight and left him thinking I'd take you back and support you, then think again.

"Until I figure out what this amnesia story is and where Ray is and what has happened to my property, then you can stay right here. As you say, you can't remember what skills you have to support yourself and you have no other place to live, so I think you'll stay right here where everything is provided for you."

"Better the enemy you see than the enemy you don't?"

David looked surprised at her statement. "Exactly!"

"Well, let me tell you this. I'm not your enemy. Maybe I was, before, although I have no idea why. Now I'm just trying to get through each day. I can't think of anything to do to you, for you, or say to you to make up for anything I've done in the past, so I'm not even going to try. I *am,* however, going to try to make up for being a neglectful mother to my son."

David's face was stern when he spoke again. "One thing I won't do, Marnie, is let you hurt Jonathan again. You've wormed your way into his heart, and he'll be hurt when you go. I have no doubt you will leave again, but there is no way I'll let you take him from me. Be careful not to make me more of an enemy than I am now by hurting Jonathan. You'll end up with nothing, nothing at all."

He started to leave and then turned back for one final word.

"You may find yourself working at the Roadhouse to support yourself after all."

Chapter 25

David was right; her old self was slowly creeping back.

Marnie sat in the chair by the window and pulled her feet up so she could wrap her arms around her knees.

For days she had been living in a state of stunned stupor, unable to fully grasp the notion that all her memories were gone and the person she had been—the person she couldn't remember—was an unlikable, untrustworthy, cheating wife.

I couldn't have been like that, I just couldn't, she had kept telling herself. Denying the possibility she could have acted the way people described was the only thing Marnie had to hold onto. The alternative was to admit they were telling the truth and take to her bed in tears. She didn't want to be that person. She would not accept it, no matter how many people told her. There must have been a reason she had acted that way—a reason no one was telling her, perhaps something they didn't know.

She had been living in fear of the truth that she was really that terrible person; she admitted it to herself. Each new day awakened the fear of finding out more hateful things about herself and the fear of what the future might hold.

This is it, she thought. *I can't sit around letting people tell me who I was or what I did. I can't spend my days worrying about what I did in the past and what is going to happen in the future. I have to take control of the only me I know—the me who's sitting here right now, not the me who ran off with a lover who stole from the family company.*

She got up and checked her pockets. Driver's license, check. Credit card and cash, check. Car keys, check. She noticed another key on the ring. *It must be to the front door,* she thought, *or else the back door. I have to be able to get back into the house.*

Picking up the jacket she had tossed on the bed, she hurried down the stairs and out the front door. *I've got to get away from here for a while.* She slid into the driver's seat of the Mustang she had left parked in the circle drive. It was tempting to release some of the tension by driving the car to its limit, but common sense prevailed. *That's all I need, a speeding ticket—one more thing to hold over my head.* Retracing the path she drove earlier, Marnie found her way back to the mall. This time she drove the length of the parking lot until she found the main entrance and a parking place nearby. She mentally cursed the part of her brain that earlier led her to park in the same spot she had used when she ran away with Ray.

Entering the wide corridor, she searched until she found a store directory at the first intersection. Locating a toy store, she proceeded down the busy thoroughfare, ignoring all other shops along the way.

"Marnie! *Marnie!*"

It took a few seconds before it registered in her brain that someone was calling her name. When she slowed her steps, a buxom blonde with a large rose tattoo above her left breast caught up to her.

"Hey! Where've you been, Marnie? I haven't seen you since that party at Eddie's place. Man, that was some scene, wasn't it? How've you been?"

Marnie had given no thought to running into someone who knew her and was thrown off guard by this woman who was obviously acquainted with her.

"Er . . . I've been sick. Really sick," was all she could think of.

"Gosh, that's too bad. You do look a little under the

weather. Or it might be because I'm not used to seeing you with no makeup on. You goin' shopping?"

"Yes, I have to buy some things for my son, and I'm in a hurry. Bye," Marnie said as she resumed walking the direction of the toy store. She might have come across as rude, but at this point, she didn't care. She felt quite sure her old self wouldn't care if she was rude to someone or not, and this Marnie didn't care if she was friendly with the woman or not either. She knew she was never going back to any party scene or associate with the people who did.

Once she found the toy store, she spent an hour browsing the aisles, looking for things that would be both entertaining and educational. Wishing she had paid more attention to the things he already had and asked him more about what he liked, she decided to buy only a few toys. She didn't want to bombard him with things, but to find more to challenge him and spark his creativity and learning. The choices he had at home seemed quite limited.

She picked out a dinosaur puzzle, animal dominoes, a rug that laid out the streets of a town, a set of buildings that went with the rug, and tiny people who worked in the buildings.

With those purchases made, she retraced her steps toward the entrance, which led her through the food court. Aromas assailed her from every direction, and her stomach reminded her it was well past lunchtime and she had only eaten toast and juice for breakfast.

She bought a large slice of pizza and a soda and took a seat at a small table half-hidden behind a potted tree. She had only eaten a few bites when a man approached her.

"Well, hello there. Long time no see." He was dressed in a suit and tie. Marnie assumed he was a businessman, but the way he leered at her made her think he was a pervert.

"Remember me? Lonnie?" he said when she didn't answer his first greeting.

"No. No, I don't remember you."

"Aw come on now, Marnie. You can't have forgotten old Lonnie, not after the good time we had."

"I said I don't remember you, and I don't want to." She reacted quickly by gathering her purchases in one hand, throwing the rest of her lunch in a trash container, and striding decisively toward the exit.

The possibility she might run into people who knew her hadn't occurred to her, but it couldn't be helped. It was either stay home, imprisoned by the fear of encountering people from her past, or brace herself for such encounters and face the world.

Marnie had intended to go to the library next, but she decided to put that off until another day. She was anxious to get home and present Jonathan with the things she bought for him. She was looking forward to playing with him, teaching him how to play dominoes, and letting him show her the proper way to work a puzzle. She was smiling at the thought when she pulled into the garage.

Chapter 26

Marnie was humming as she browsed through the clothing in her closet. The hour she spent with Jonathan had lifted her spirits. He was thrilled with the items she had purchased. She taught him about matching the animals on the large cardboard cards, and they played several hands of animal dominoes. After the game, she spread the rug on the floor, and they discussed the proper arrangement for the buildings.

"See, we can't put the fire station too close to the school because the siren on the fire truck would be too loud for the children studying," he reasoned.

"That's good thinking!"

"Let's put it here, not far from the houses, so if they catch fire, the firemen can come in a hurry."

"Where should we put the hospital?"

Together they arranged and rearranged until it suited Jonathan, and when she left to dress for dinner, he was busy running his cars up and down the streets of his pretend town. She made a mental note to be sure he had a small fire truck, police car, and ambulance to use with the set.

After a shower, she was again left with the problem of finding something suitable to wear. "Tomorrow I'm going to start weeding out clothes I'll never wear again," she said to herself. "Maybe then I can see what I have that isn't too short, too tight, or too low cut."

She finally decided on a voile skirt printed with blue and green swirls and lined with coordinating fabric gathered on an elastic band. She liked the way it flared and moved when she walked. With it she donned a silk and cashmere sweater. In a drawer full of costume jewelry she found a long silver chain that she added to the costume, along with silver bracelets and earrings. When she looked at herself in the mirror, the feeling she got made her hum some more of the tune that filled her head.

When she entered the dining room, she found Mrs. Grady scurrying around setting food on the table and muttering to herself.

"Good evening, Mrs. Grady. I thought I was late, but I see I'm the first one here."

"Good evening, Miss Marnie."

Marnie noticed the table was only set for two.

"Should I not have come?" she asked, thinking Ruth or David might have banned her from the dinner table.

"What's that? Oh . . . oh, no, you're fine. It's Miss Ruth who's not coming. She's decided to eat in her room from now on. Mary will take her food to her and then serve you and Mr. David."

"That makes a lot more work on you."

"Not me, it don't. Mary's the one 'ats got to see to her majesty's whims, she is," Mrs. Grady retorted.

"Am I the reason she isn't coming to the table?"

"Who's to know? She's been terrible flighty since Mr. Robert and Mr. John died. Miss Celeste can get her out of the house, and she does go to the country club some or out to eat with her women friends, but she's spendin' more and more time in her room."

"I just hate to be the cause of more work for you and Mary and Alice. Everyone did so much for me when I was sick in bed, and I want you to know I appreciate it, Mrs. Grady."

"Luv, that's one thing you always done right, never tried to cause us any more work, and always told us thank you. Alice says it's 'cause you come from working folks yourself, and not from money." She headed back toward the kitchen but stopped and faced Marnie. "I'm not saying everything you did was right, mind ye'. You ran with an awful wild crowd, if someone hasn't already told you, and you didn't treat Mr. David or your sweet little tyke like you ought to have, but you tried not to make any extra work on the help, and you always said thank you. Your mama raised you right, that way, at least." With that she pushed through the swinging door.

Marnie wondered if she would be eating alone. She put her hands on the back of her chair to pull it out when she heard David on the stairs, and within moments he came rushing into the room.

"I'm sorry I'm late." He was gasping for breath. "I got to playing with Jonathan and let the time get away from me."

"That's easy to do," Marnie said.

"Mother's not here yet?"

"Mrs. Grady said Ruth is taking her dinner in her room from now on."

"Oh, for heaven's sake," David said irritably as he pulled out Marnie's chair for her. "Well, I'm not bending over backward for her this time. Let her eat there if that's what she wants. She'll come out soon enough when she wants to know what's going on in the house and at the plant."

"What do you mean?" Marnie asked as she spread the napkin across her lap.

David passed Marnie the plate of chicken as he spoke. "When she gets mad about something or doesn't get her way, she goes to her room and pouts." He took the plate back and served himself. "She's mad you're still here, that I haven't thrown you out on the street."

"Well, I've wondered about that myself," she responded as she spooned some mashed potatoes onto her plate.

"You said it yourself. Keep your enemies close." He grinned, so she didn't know what to think about that statement.

They ate in silence for a few minutes before David spoke. "You did a good job picking things for Jonathan. He's excited about the things you bought. I had to stay and discuss his town for a while, then play a few hands of dominoes. That's why I was late to dinner."

"Yes, I played with him, too. I enjoy seeing him so happy."

David stopped eating and looked at Marnie. When he spoke, his voice was low and quiet. "I should have done that before—bought him some educational toys. Now that I look at it, he has, or had, very little to play with. Mrs. Tucker is good to watch him, but she takes no initiative in pointing out things he needs. She doesn't like to drive, she doesn't like to shop, and she doesn't take him to places outside the house very often.

"On the weekends I try to take him out to the park or to the movies, but I probably should take him shopping sometimes, too, so he can pick out things he would like."

"Has he ever been in a toy store?"

"Come to think of it, he hasn't. I'm sure you never took him, nor did I, and Mother surely wouldn't."

"Why do you say Ruth wouldn't?" Marnie asked, refusing to get sucked back into what a bad mother she had been.

"Jonathan may be my son and her grandson, but he's your son, too, and that offends her sensibilities. She found Mrs. Tucker when you became overwhelmed with taking care of a baby. In her mind, that is the limit of her grandmotherly duties."

"She doesn't play with him? Read to him? Love him?" Her voice almost broke with the thought of Jonathan's grandmother not loving him, and all because of her.

"No. None of that."

They were quiet for a while as they ate.

"Is there anything I can get for you?" Mary asked as she entered from the kitchen.

David glanced at Marnie and then answered, "No, thank you, Mary. I think we're ready for dessert now."

Mary brought individual bowls of banana pudding and started to clear the dirty plates and platters from the table. Marnie waited for Mary to leave before speaking.

"You know, there's no reason for two people to work late just to serve our supper. I'm going to try to come down earlier to set the table, and I can carry in the serving bowls, too. If we need something else, I'll get up and get it. There's no need to have Mrs. Grady and Mary to wait on us."

David raised his eyebrows, but when Mary returned, he said, "Just leave the rest, Mary, and go on home. We'll take care of the dishes."

She looked startled.

"Is my mother settled for the evening?"

"Yes, sir."

"Then carry those on into the kitchen and leave them. We'll take it from here."

He probably thinks I'm putting on a show. If that's the case, he's got another thing coming. When they finished dessert, she rose and started gathering the remaining dishes. He picked up the rest and followed her into the kitchen.

Together they rinsed the dishes and put them in the dishwasher. David reached under the sink and retrieved the detergent and filled the dispenser.

"So you know how to do this," Marnie commented, as she searched the front of the dishwasher for the right buttons.

"You bet. I do this on the weekends."

"Did I ever help you?"

"Not that I can recall. As soon as you were through eating dinner you got up and left the room, and you were seldom around on the weekends, unless you were trying to wheedle me into going to some party or another."

"Did I ever succeed? Did you go?"

"Not to the parties you wanted to go to. We went to ones my friends gave, but you thought those were boring."

Marnie remembered what the blonde woman at the mall had said about a party and shuddered. She didn't want to think about the kind of parties she might have attended.

"Tomorrow is Saturday. Why don't you spend it with us for a change?"

A thrill of pleasure shot through her.

"There's nothing I'd like more," she answered.

"Mrs. Tucker reminded me again this evening that Jonathan needs some new clothes. I thought I'd take him shopping, and of course, do some fun things."

"I'd love that," she replied. "Do I usually join you two on Saturdays?"

"No. This will be the first time."

As they parted and she went upstairs to her room, a broad smile filled her face and she was humming again. This had turned out to be a wonderful day.

Chapter 27

Marnie followed the scent of bacon to the kitchen. When she pushed open the swinging door, she saw Jonathan sitting at the island and David at the range flipping a pancake high into the air.

"Oops," he said as it landed in a pile instead of flat on the griddle. Jonathan was chortling at the failed exploit, and Marnie laughed aloud, too, more at Jonathan's gaiety than her husband's act. Father and son turned in unison at the sound of her laughter.

"Good morning!" David said, and Jonathan echoed him.

"Good morning, gentlemen. I didn't expect to find a cook in the kitchen this morning."

"Daddy's a good cook," Jonathan offered. "He just can't throw the pancakes up in the air and have them come down right!"

"Let me make up some more batter, and I'll show you what kind of cook I am," David said, reaching for a box of mix. "I don't make them from scratch," he said to Marnie, who had come up beside him. "Hungry Jack makes them better than I can."

"Yeah, that's what I always use," Marnie said, then looked at David at the same time he looked at her. "Why did I say that? Did I used to make the pancakes?"

"No. Never. Why *did* you say that?"

"I don't have a clue." She turned away. "Maybe my mom and I made them when I was a kid. I don't know."

David shook his head. "You remember the most useless information." He threw Marnie a playful smile. "One of these times it's going to be something important, and when the dam breaks, you'll remember everything."

"I hope so," Marnie murmured, but she wasn't too sure she wanted to remember *everything*.

As David poured more pancakes onto the griddle, Marnie went to the pantry and searched the shelves.

"What are you looking for?" he asked.

"These," she said as she came out of the pantry holding a bag. Returning to the stove, she opened the bag and took out a handful of chocolate chips. Carefully she arranged them on a pancake. "Let them sink down into the batter before you flip that one."

David was grinning when he delivered the smiley face pancake to Jonathan, who laughed when he saw it. "I'm eating his eye," he announced as he took a bite. "Now I'm eating his nose."

"The bacon is on that platter," David said, pointing. "Do you want some pancakes?"

"You bet I do!"

"Do you want smiley face ones?" Jonathan asked.

"No, I think I want plain ones this morning. Why don't you eat those while they're hot, and I'll make my own?" she said to David.

"What? And take away my job as chef?" David bantered.

"I'm eating his mouth," Jonathan declared.

"My goodness, what a charming little scene. So domestic," drawled a voice from the doorway.

David's smile disappeared. "Celeste, how did you get in?"

"Your mother gave me a key, David. She thought I should have one in case I was needed. You know, to help with Jonathan or something."

"We didn't call for any help, so what are you doing here?"

"Darling, don't be mad! We're going out for the day, your mother and I. She needs someone to be her friend. She feels so . . . alone."

He didn't comment on his mother's feelings but rather tersely said, "She's in her room. You know the way," and turned back to his cooking.

"If you needed someone to fix your breakfast, you could have called me. I make wonderful breakfasts. You do remember, don't you?"

"I prefer my own cooking, Celeste. You and Mother have a nice day. Goodbye."

Celeste glared at him, then turned on her stilettos and left the room.

Marnie felt it wise to keep her thoughts to herself, so she went to the refrigerator to find something to drink.

"Jonathan, do you want milk or juice?"

"Milk, please."

She placed a glass in front of him and poured it about half full. "That's so it'll be easier not to spill. Tell me if you want more."

David looked at her oddly. "That's a good idea. He spills it quite often."

"And what do you want to drink?"

"I have coffee right here, but I'll take a glass of milk, too."

She grinned. "Should I make yours half full, too?"

"Maybe you ought to. Sometimes I spill stuff when I get upset."

"Why are you upset, Daddy?" Jonathan asked.

"Little pitchers," Marnie said softly as she poured the milk.

"Because I can't flip a pancake right," David answered.

When breakfast was eaten and the kitchen straightened, the trio proceeded upstairs to brush their teeth and fetch their jackets.

"It's a beautiful day, Jonathan. Let's get out of the house," David said to his son.

"Can we go to the park, please, Daddy? We haven't been there in a long time 'cause it's been so cold."

"We'll go there first, for a little while, but then we're going to go shopping for some new clothes for you. Mrs.

Tucker tells me you're growing so fast all your jeans and shirts are too small."

Jonathan was amenable to the suggestion, and they drove to the park where Marnie had found herself that first day. They parked at the curb, and Jonathan raced to the climbing bars.

"Come this way," David said, taking Marnie by the elbow. "Let's walk back over where you remember standing. Maybe now that the snow is gone, we can find your cell phone or wallet."

They looked all over with no more luck than they had the first time they searched. By this time, Jonathan had grown tired of climbing and approached them.

"Daddy, can we go to the other park? There aren't any kids here, and the stuff at the other park is funner."

"OK, Sport. We can do that."

After driving to the other side of town, they reached a neighborhood with newer homes. Ranch style houses and two story colonials mingled with more modern dwellings of stone and glass. They passed a sprawling school on the way. When they reached the park, a throng of children was playing on the swings, teeter-totters, and slides. Jonathan hurried off to a small merry-go-round where an older child pushed it before hopping on himself.

Marnie and David sat on a bench where they could watch the action.

"I'm so glad he could get out of the house today."

"Yes. The snow and cold this winter has kept us inside on the weekends. He deserves to get out and play," David answered, hooking his elbows over the back of the bench.

"I think I'd go stir-crazy being cooped up in the house day after day."

"Maybe that's why you never stayed home," he replied sharply.

"Maybe. But why didn't I take him out with me?"

"Because he would cramp your style? Maybe because

you didn't want people to see you as a mother? I don't know, Marnie. I don't know why you don't, or didn't, love your son."

"I love him now, and that's all I know."

They were quiet for a while, watching Jonathan move from the merry-go-round to the slide, taking turns with the other children. Nothing more could be said about Marnie's past that hadn't been repeated over the last few days.

"This looks like a pleasant neighborhood," Marnie commented. "Nice homes and lots of children."

"It is. I lived in this neighborhood before my father and uncle died."

"I think you or Alice once said something about your moving back home then."

"Yes. My mother just couldn't be alone, so I sold my condo and moved back in with her."

"That was good of you."

He raised one eyebrow as if to question her meaning, so she tried to reassure him. "Really. It's what you should have done if she needed you."

As Jonathan ran to the teeter-totters with another boy about his size, Marnie turned her face up to the sun and closed her eyes. "This feels so good," she said.

When she opened her eyes, she noticed David was staring at her, but he turned away quickly.

Searching for a neutral subject, she asked. "The school we drove by on this street, is that where Jonathan will start to school?"

"No, his school will be on the other side of town, closer to the house." He stood and reached a hand out to her. "It's time we did some shopping." He called out, "Jonathan, it's time to go. Come on."

Jonathan hurried to them. "Daddy, that's my friend Ricky I was playing with. He wants to know if I can come to this park again sometime."

"Someday, Jonathan. I'll try to bring you again someday."

Chapter 28

When they walked out of the department store, David's arms were filled with bags. He had purchased everything they could think Jonathan might need: jeans, shirts, socks, underwear, pajamas, and a lightweight jacket. Marnie was stunned by the amount of money David spent without comment.

Why should I be surprised? she thought. *He is obviously a wealthy man from a wealthy family. From the looks of my closet, I must have spent money the same way.*

"Next comes shoes, buddy," David told the boy who was skipping along beside them.

Marnie was trying to hold his hand, but it was a difficult task with his jumping and bouncing at every step.

"I'll tell you what, Jonathan. If you'll walk calmly and not jump around so your mother can hold your hand, we'll buy you a special treat."

Jonathan immediately slowed down to a normal pace. He looked up at Marnie for a few seconds and then reached to take her hand.

"What treat?" he asked.

"You'll see. I have to see if you're going to behave," David said in a solemn voice.

They entered a store that sold athletic shoes. Jonathan's eyes widened when he saw the vast assortment of shoes. The salesman measured his feet, and when they left, he was wearing a new pair of shoes and carrying another.

"Now, let's go get you a prize for being so good," David said.

When they entered the toy store, Jonathan's face lit up.

"I've never seen so many toys," he said. "I didn't know there were this many toys in the whole world."

"This is where I bought the things I gave you yesterday," Marnie told him.

Marnie felt like they had looked at every toy in the shop. She figured David had had enough shopping when he said, "It's time to make a choice, Sport. What shall we buy?"

Jonathan hemmed and hawed, unable to decide among all the riches before him.

"How about some more parts for your town?" Marnie suggested. "Like a fire truck and ambulance and police car?"

"Yeah! And how 'bout some trees? I don't have any trees," Jonathan said.

Choices made and paid for, they exited the store and started back along the wide corridor.

"Tell you what," David said. "Why don't we stop in the food court and get some lunch? Maybe some pizza."

"Pizza! Hurray!" Jonathan exclaimed.

"No, not there. Let's go somewhere else," Marnie said.

"Where would you suggest then?"

"Anywhere. Anywhere but here."

When they reached the car, David clicked the remote to unlock it and told Jonathan to get in the backseat while he and Marnie put the packages in the trunk. Once Jonathan was out of earshot, David asked in a low voice, "You want to tell me what that was all about? Did you remember something else?"

"No, it wasn't that. Yesterday, when I was eating lunch in the food court, some man came up to me. He said he knew me."

"And you didn't know him." It was a statement, not a question.

"No, I didn't know him, but he was smarmy. I didn't want him around me."

"Smarmy? What do you mean?"

"He was dressed like a businessman, in a suit and tie, but he was . . . oily looking. Slick. Not to be trusted. *Smarmy*!" She placed her packages in the trunk. As she started toward the front of the car, she heard David snicker. When she looked at him, she saw he was grinning. "It's not funny."

"In a way it is. You meet someone you knew, maybe intimately, and you don't even recognize him. I'll bet that was a blow to his ego." He closed the trunk. "What did you do?"

"I told him to leave me alone, and I threw my lunch away and left."

"Good for you!" David said. Then he leaned over and kissed her lightly on the lips.

Marnie's heart fluttered. It took a lot of self-discipline to keep from deepening the kiss. It was short. Much too short.

David treated Jonathan to hamburgers and fries, a treat reserved for weekends out, as Ruth forbade fast food in her house. They also had sodas, another special treat. "What should we do this afternoon?" David asked when they had finished eating.

"How 'bout min-min-er golf?" Jonathan asked.

"I think miniature golf is still closed for the winter. That will be good to do when it gets warmer. Would you like to see what's playing at the movie theaters?"

Jonathan excitedly agreed. There were several choices of children's movies, and it was hard for Jonathan to settle on one, but he finally did.

Every step of the way, every minute of the afternoon, Marnie relived the kiss. *It was only a peck,* she kept telling herself. *It didn't mean anything. He doesn't love me anymore, if he ever did. I've messed my marriage up too much to ever salvage it.* Despite her attempt to convince herself it was nothing, she couldn't stop thinking about his lips on hers and the thrill that had run through her—was still running through her.

How can I forget when he keeps touching me? she thought. It seemed like he had started putting his hand on her back every time they were close. It was driving her crazy. She didn't dare make eye contact, certain she would appear love-struck if she did. *Thank heavens Jonathan is sitting between us,* she thought as they watched the movie. *We would have to share an armrest if we sat next to each other.*

Marnie spent so much time thinking about David she didn't realize the movie had ended. When they left the theater, the sun was low on the western horizon.

"Time to go home," David said. "Or would you rather eat supper somewhere?" he asked Marnie.

"We'd better go on home. We have a sleepy boy on our hands," she replied as they reached the car.

"I'm not sleepy," Jonathan said, as he yawned.

On the way home, Marnie tried to keep Jonathan awake by talking about the movie. She didn't want to admit that it also kept her from having to keep up a conversation with David. A few minutes later they pulled into the garage at home.

"Why don't you take Jonathan upstairs to put his new clothes and toys away while I see what there is for supper," she said to David. "And be sure he washes his hands and face before he comes back down."

Marnie found leftover chicken from the night before, along with a bowl of potato salad and gelatin with fruit. She put it all on the breakfast bar and was putting the finishing touches on the place settings when David and Jonathan arrived.

Supper was a silent affair. While Marnie and David ate, Jonathan struggled to stay awake.

"I think that's enough. His face will be in his plate any second now," Marnie said.

David lifted Jonathan from the bar stool, and he was asleep by the time his head reached his father's shoulder. Marnie trailed them upstairs and helped David get the sleeping boy out of his clothes and into pajamas.

Together they returned to the kitchen, put the remaining food away, and loaded the dishwasher. Few words were spoken between them as they tended to their duties. With the last crumb wiped away, Marnie hung the cloth over the sink divider and stared out the window. She felt so awkward she didn't know what to do next. Her attraction to David was powerful, yet she knew he didn't feel the same thing toward her. She had ruined their relationship with her infidelity and disloyalty. The kiss meant nothing to him, she was sure—nothing at all.

"This day has worn me out just like it did Jonathan," she said. "I think I'll go up and take a hot bath and get to bed early. Maybe read for a while." Now she wouldn't have to sit around and make awkward conversation.

"That's a good idea. I think I'll do the same." Together they went up the massive staircase.

"I'll just check on Jonathan to see he's sleeping OK," she told him.

"I'll go with you. I like to check on him last thing every night."

Together, they watched their sleeping boy. Marnie leaned over and kissed his forehead. When she straightened up, David was just inches away. He put his arms around her and pressed his lips to hers.

When he finally released her, Marnie was reeling, but David set her away and took a step back. He looked as stunned as she felt.

"Good night," he said, as he hurried from the room.

Chapter 29

Marnie tried to relax by taking the hot bath she had mentioned to David. Drawing a tub of soothing water liberally laced with bubble bath, she lit the candles that sat on the rim and placed the poufy bath pillow at one end. The relaxing water and atmosphere should have calmed her, but it didn't.

Bubbles tickled her chin as she sank deeper into the water. *What is going on in his mind? The first kiss was only a throwaway for him, I'm sure of it. It meant nothing to him, even if it did shake me to my toes. But the second one! That one was mind-bending, muscle-melting, can't stand up, stupendous! And then he just walked away. What's with that?*

She had been told she did not love her husband. She had used pregnancy to trap him into marriage because she wanted his money. She didn't love him. Her repeated infidelity proved that. She and her lover schemed to get more money out of David via a son she planned to use for ransom.

But all of this didn't line up with the way she felt. She didn't understand why she wouldn't be in love with David. He was kind; a loving father; generous, even with his wayward wife; handsome; and a great kisser. There most certainly was passion between them, as this day had proven.

The stories she had been told were from other people's viewpoints. What Marnie didn't know was her side of the story. There was bound to be a lot they weren't telling her. *I know I wouldn't marry just for money*, she reasoned. *There had to be more to it than that. And maybe I didn't cheat on him. Maybe that was just the idle gossip of people who were jealous because I married the boss. Maybe Ruth perpetuated those stories, spread them among her friends, and told them to David. Maybe she encouraged him to believe them because she thought my mother had an affair with her husband. Ruth wants Celeste as a daughter-in-law instead of me, and she'll say anything to make that happen.*

I've been beating myself up because I thought all those things about me were true, but maybe they aren't. Maybe they're stories that have gotten twisted every which way and blown out of proportion.

The water cooled, so Marnie got out of the tub and dried herself. Wrapping the oversized towel around her, she rummaged through a drawer for something to wear for the night. Ordinarily, she put on a pair of pajamas like the ones Alice had dressed her in when she stumbled home that first night, weak and sick. She hoped, though, that her husband's kiss might be a prelude to more, and she might have a visitor.

She donned a silky pink gown, sheer and willowy, and misted herself lightly with lily-of-the-valley scent. All preparations completed, she went to bed. Alone. And tossed. And turned. Hours went by. Sleep did not come. Neither did David. Anger did, however.

What did he think he was doing, kissing me like that and then leaving? He's a tease! He's my husband, for heaven's sake! He knows he can come to my bed, and that kiss was proof he was thinking about it, at least. So where is he? How can he treat me like this? Was it some sort of repayment for the way he thinks I treated him?

She fell asleep for only a few minutes before she was awake again, agonizing over the situation. Finally, she threw the covers back and got out of bed. Determined to not give in to the desire for her husband, she had to find something to do. She didn't want to wander around the big house in the middle of the night, so she entered her closet dressing room and put on a warm robe.

"I might as well get to this now," she said, as she started through the clothes on the rack.

A pile of discarded clothes grew on the floor. Out went the mini-skirts. Out went the shirt with "bitch" written across the front, along with all the tees she judged to be a size too small. Dresses that were as short as the mini-skirts topped the stack. Dresses and blouses with a plunging neckline started a new pile. A few things were added to the growing stack that were acceptable in style and size, but Marnie was puzzled as to why she would ever buy the particular color.

The last rack held the evening dresses. "Surely I didn't attend this many parties," she muttered as she discarded dress after dress she judged suitable for a teenaged exhibitionist, "and if I did, why in the world would I wear something like this? No wonder men came sniffing around. It's like these clothes say, 'I'm a tramp, come get me'," she said, dejectedly. "No wonder people formed a bad opinion of me when I dressed this way."

It was four o'clock in the morning before she was tired enough for bed. The shoes and items in the drawers could wait for another time. She drifted off to sleep quickly, again thinking she must have earned the reputation people thought of her.

It was after 10:00 a.m. before she woke up. She dressed in jeans and a sweater and headed to the kitchen, looking in at the empty playroom on the way. David had already fetched Jonathan and fed him breakfast. *If I were a good mother, I would have been up earlier and checked in on him already*. It was another thing she let herself feel guilty about.

She fixed herself a bowl of cereal and milk. After she ate, she rinsed the bowl and put it in the dishwasher. She might as well get it over with—facing David had to be done. She found David and Jonathan in the TV room. Jonathan was working his new puzzle on the table in front of the window, and David was on the sofa reading the newspaper.

"Good morning," she said. Jonathan rushed to her and hugged her knees, his usual form of greeting.

"Good morning," David said. "I was beginning to wonder if you were going to spend the day in your room."

"No. I had trouble sleeping, so when I finally fell asleep I overslept."

He gave her a piercing look but said nothing about her sleep habits.

"It's raining today, so we thought we'd stay in," he remarked.

"I'm working the puzzle you gave me," Jonathan said. "Come see."

He pulled her toward his project, where she admired his puzzle-working skills. She vacillated between sitting down with Jonathan and joining David, when he asked, "Want part of the paper?"

"Sure." She took the sections he held out to her and sat down on the other end of the sofa.

It had never occurred to her that reading the local paper might be an excellent way to jog her memory about the town and the people in it, so she studied each article and picture, but none of it seemed familiar. Soon, she stopped trying to find anything that sparked recall and started reading articles that interested her.

"Next month there is going to be a big exhibition of paintings and blown glass at the Center for the Arts," she remarked. "Could you show me how to get there?" she asked.

"You're looking at the Centerview newspaper," he answered, "not the local paper. Does the exhibition interest you?" David looked at her quizzically.

"Yes, it does. Shouldn't it?"

"I just never heard you express an interest in the arts before." His paper lay unread for a few moments. "We'll try to go, if you want to. It's only about an hour from here. Remind me next month." He went back to reading.

He must expect I'll still be around in a month, she thought. *At least he's not going to throw me out before then.*

When she came to the book review section, she folded it so that a book that sounded like a good read was visible and placed the paper on the table at her end of the couch. David got up and started to gather the papers scattered about the couch and floor.

"Are you through reading all this?" he asked.

"Yes, but don't throw away this one," she said, indicating the article on the table.

"What's that?"

"It's a book review. I plan to go to the library this week and get a card. I thought I'd see if they have it—maybe check it out when I get Jonathan some books."

Again, David gave her an odd look. She assumed she hadn't made a point about liking to read before now. *Maybe he hasn't been paying attention to what I'm really like. Maybe he's been so angry about being 'trapped' into marriage he's ignored the real Marnie. Well, too bad. It's time for him to face up to the woman he married.*

"It's time for lunch, Sport," he said to Jonathan. "I'm going to the kitchen to fix us some sandwiches. You go wash up." He turned to Marnie. "Come to the kitchen with me. I need to talk to you."

She followed him into the kitchen, both dreading and wondering what he had to say.

"I want to apologize for last night," he said, leaning against the counter and crossing his arms. "I should never have kissed you."

Marnie closed her eyes. *So he doesn't want me. The kiss means nothing if he regrets doing it.*

"We both know this marriage isn't working," he said.

I know nothing of the sort. That's just what you've told me, she thought, but she couldn't bring herself to voice it aloud.

"So, I have no business kissing you like that. I've already admitted you have a strong sexual pull, but I have no intention of letting you sucker me back into the situation we were in before." He straightened, turned toward the cabinet, and started removing plates. "Our marriage is over. I'm not going to end up in bed with you again."

Chapter 30

Marnie's life quickly developed a pattern. Each day, she arose, dressed, and joined Jonathan and Mrs. Tucker for breakfast in the kitchen. Afterwards, she spent time with her son, playing a game or working a puzzle. She read and reread the half-dozen books he possessed.

By Thursday the rain that had plagued the earlier part of the week had disappeared, and the day was sunny and warm. She went to the library and signed up for a card so she could check out books. Filling out her name, address, and phone number, plus the name of a relative who lived in the same town, seemed odd to her. Of course she put David's name, but she wasn't sure he would vouch for her if called. The form asked for a non-relative reference also, but she didn't have one. She thought about putting Alice's name down, but she didn't know Alice's last name, much less her address and phone number. When she returned the form to the desk, she told the woman she couldn't think of anyone to put down for a reference. When the woman read the application, she smiled at Marnie and said, "Oh, that's all right, Mrs. Barrett. Everyone knows where to find you."

Marnie browsed through the children's section and picked out half a dozen books she thought Jonathan might like. She chose one about dinosaurs, a picture book about big trucks, and several books with stories that sounded interesting.

Going to the section marked "new arrivals," she found the book that had been reviewed in Sunday's newspaper and added it to her pile. She then searched the card file on the computer for a book about amnesia. She scanned the shelves and picked one that seemed simple enough to understand.

Jonathan was thrilled with the books and fascinated by the idea there was a place where one could borrow books. Marnie explained that they could keep them for two weeks but then she would have to take them back to the library.

"I can get more books when I take these back," she explained to him. "And if you get tired of these, I can return them early and borrow others."

Reading became a more enjoyable part of their daily routine. After lunch most afternoons, Marnie settled on the couch in the TV room and read to Jonathan, who snuggled close to her and looked at the pictures as she read. They had discussions about dinosaurs, earthmoving equipment, and the plots in the books she had chosen for him.

In the late afternoon, Jonathan returned to Mrs. Tucker's care, and Marnie retreated to her bedroom to dress for supper with David. She changed from jeans into a skirt or dress. Since ridding the racks of clothing she considered to be unacceptable, she didn't have many options, but she didn't mind wearing the few things over and over. She liked the pink knit dress and the swirly blue and green skirt. Lately, she had started wearing trousers and a silk blouse with a scarf or necklaces as accessories. She was able to put together several outfits with the separates she kept.

After showering and dressing, she took a few minutes to read the novel or study what the book on amnesia had to say. She wasn't learning anything new, since it said the same thing Doctor Means had told her. Namely, amnesia could be caused by a lot of things, most commonly trauma, either physical or emotional, and the memory usually returned at some point.

By five-thirty, she was in the kitchen helping Mrs. Grady. She set the dining room table with places for David and herself. She seldom saw Ruth, who no longer ate supper with them and left the room without speaking any time Marnie walked in. Marnie helped carry the bowls and platters of food into the dining room right at six o'clock so it would still be hot when David arrived to eat. She was finally able to convince Mrs. Grady and Mary she could get anything they needed, including the dessert left on the counter for them, and she could clear the table, put the dishes in the dishwasher, and run it if it was full.

One afternoon, Marnie was dragging her two bags of clothing along the hall. Having determined they were too large to fit in the dumbwaiter, she approached the top of the stairs when David came bounding up.

"What in the world are you doing?" he asked.

"Getting rid of clothes I'm not going to wear anymore," she panted, out of breath from trying to fit them into the dumbwaiter.

"Where are you going with them?"

"I'm giving them to Mary to take to her church thrift shop. They outfit people who need clothing and don't have money to buy any."

David doubled over with laughter. "I can't imagine anyone who needs clothing bad enough to wear any of your castoffs," he said. "Sequins and miniskirts and tee shirts with sexy sayings on the front." He chuckled. "And what does that leave you to wear? Are you planning on a whole new wardrobe?"

"I have plenty to wear, thank you very much," she tartly replied and pulled the sacks, bumping, down the stairs.

Marnie entered the dining room for supper wearing dark gray wool slacks and a lighter gray silk blouse. The blouse plunged a bit deeper than what she was comfortable wearing, but she liked the color and style, so she kept it from the discard pile. She used a colorful scarf to pull the collar together a little higher.

"You look very nice tonight."

"Thank you," she said, glancing down at what she was wearing.

They ate in companionable silence until dessert.

"You look nice every night. I'm sorry I haven't told you before," David said.

She patted her mouth with her napkin. Unable to find anything more appropriate to say, she simply repeated, "Thank you."

They cleared the table together, as had become the custom, and David retired to the TV room while Marnie finished wiping off the counters. Since he had been thoughtful enough to compliment her on her clothes, she decided to say good night before heading upstairs. When she arrived in the west hall, she heard the sounds of the TV, and when she got closer, she heard David cheering. She watched the TV from the doorway for a few minutes.

"Is that the Suns playing?" she asked.

David turned to her, startled by her appearance and by what she had said.

"Yes, it's the Suns. I'm surprised you know them. I didn't know you followed basketball."

"I didn't know I did, either," she replied, "but I recognize them."

On the screen, a ball circled the hoop, falling outside, and the crowd moaned. Marnie moaned along with them. "Aww, bummer," she said. David continued to stare at her, the game forgotten.

Finally, he patted the couch beside him. "Come and watch with me." She settled herself at the other end of the sofa and became involved in the game, cheering or moaning as the Suns and their opponent battled on the court. Although David was watching the play on the screen, Marnie noticed that part of his attention had settled on her. At last the game was over. He switched off the TV and turned to Marnie.

Chapter 31

"As far as I know, you've lived here since you were a small child. And I've never known you to have an interest in basketball. But you immediately recognized the Phoenix Suns when you saw them on television."

"I know. That's weird, isn't it?"

"Maybe not so weird. Ray is a big basketball fan. One of the companies the detective suspects he might have been going to sell the stolen prototype and plans to is located in Phoenix. There must be a reason you recognized the Suns from a brief glimpse of them on television. Maybe that's where you've been."

"I have no idea why," Marnie replied. "When I saw them, I just knew who they were."

"Ray is an avid follower of the sport. He always talked about it at the office and seldom missed a game on television. He even pays extra for the sports channel that carries the games and invites coworkers to his apartment to watch with him."

"Maybe I watched games with him."

"Maybe," David reluctantly agreed. "But I can't see you doing that. The private detective I hired to trace Ray's tracks obtained Ray's cell phone records, and they showed calls to several people connected with Barrett's competitors. One of those competitors is located in Phoenix. Think, Marnie. Does Phoenix call up any memories for you?"

She sat quietly for a while and then shook her head. "In a way it seems familiar, but nothing specific comes to mind. Alice said she thought my mother and I might have moved here from Phoenix. Maybe I feel a connection to the city because of that."

"Or maybe you two flew to Phoenix so Ray could meet with someone, and while you were there, you attended a Suns' game. Does that ring a bell?"

She leaned her head against the back of the sofa and closed her eyes. "Somehow I remember being at a basketball game, but when or where I don't know. I can even visualize seeing the Suns playing, but I don't know when or who I was with." She sat up straight and opened her eyes. "I'm trying so hard there's a chance I might be making the whole thing up in my head—it may be my imagination along with seeing basketball on TV."

The next day Marnie's thoughts kept coming back to basketball and the memories that had started to flicker in and out of her mind. She was excited that some memories were returning, even something as trivial as attending a basketball game, but no other details about it surfaced. That evening at supper, David led the conversation back to the game and the various teams and how the basketball season was progressing.

"The Suns are having a good season this year," he said.

When Marnie agreed and mentioned the current coach by name, David's jaw dropped. Marnie looked back at him in amazement.

"Oh, my God!" she said. "How did I know that?"

"How do you know who the coach is?" David asked.

"I don't know."

"Either Ray has talked about it around you or the subject has come up in conversation."

"Either way, does that necessarily mean we went to Phoenix with your project?"

"No," he said, and slumped in his chair. "No, it doesn't. The private detective I hired, Grigsby, is at a dead end on that lead. He can't find any proof, or even a hint beyond phone calls, that Ray connected with anyone at the Phoenix company. He hasn't picked up on any rumors circulating about it."

Other than the conversations about Marnie's knowledge of basketball in general and the Phoenix Suns in particular, the week went as the previous one had. Marnie spent her days playing with Jonathan and reading to him, reading the novel from the library, and helping in the kitchen.

When Saturday arrived, David asked Jonathan at breakfast what he would like to do.

"Can we go to the library, Daddy? That's a place with lots and lots of books, and I've read the ones I have. I need some new ones."

"He wanted to go this week," Marnie explained, "but I told him I couldn't take him, that you'd have to do it. I'm sorry if I messed up your plans. That's the only thing I could think of to tell him."

"That's OK. I think the library is a good place to start the day," David responded.

Upon entering the library, Jonathan was overwhelmed by the amount of books available to him, so he chose an armload to bring home. The afternoon was spent at the neighborhood park. Marnie and David sat on a bench and continued to discuss the meaning of Marnie's knowledge of the Phoenix Suns and basketball while Jonathan played. Since she was unable to remember anything new, they let the conversation drop.

"This weather is wonderful," Marnie said, turning her face toward the sun. "I hate to stay in the house on days like this."

"I've never thought of you as an outdoor girl," David responded. "In fact . . ."

"In fact what?" Marnie opened her eyes and looked at him.

"Hmm. I just had an idea," he answered.

"What is it?"

"Never mind. I'll tell you later."

Over spaghetti and meatballs at David's favorite Italian restaurant, he said to Jonathan, "I think it's about time to open up the cabin for the year. Are you up for it, Sport?"

"Yay! Daddy, when can we go? Tomorrow?"

David laughed. "Not that soon, buddy, but maybe next week."

He focused his attention on Marnie. "We have a cabin up in the mountains. It was my father and uncle's getaway. They called it a hunting cabin, but I don't know how much hunting either of them did up there. They'd go up there and talk about business deals and profits and losses—things they didn't want to talk about around other people. It's not fancy, but it's not primitive either. There's running water, heat, a kitchen, and an indoor bathroom. Jonathan loves it up there."

"When can we go, Daddy?" Jonathan asked again.

"I'll have to call the Evertons and ask them to get it ready for us." He turned to Marnie. "Chad and Dina Everton own a little grocery store and gas station about two miles away from the cabin. They check on it for me, and they'll go air it out and see if there's been any damage from the winter weather." He turned to Jonathan. "I'll call them on Monday, Sport, and get the ball rolling. I'll let you know when we can go. It'll be a few days."

Jonathan was beside himself for the next two days. He told Marnie all about the tall mountains and the lake near the cabin. "And we can walk down to the dock and fish. I caught a fish one time, but Daddy said it wasn't big enough to keep, so I had to throw it back so it could grow some more. I can't go to the lake by myself because I'm too little, so I have to have a grownup go with me. And . . ."

Marnie was in the playroom with Jonathan and Mrs. Tucker, listening to Jonathan share the wonders of the cabin for the umpteenth time, when David arrived home early from work.

"Did you find out, Daddy? Did you?" Jonathan was jumping up and down as he asked.

"Jonathan, settle down," Mrs. Tucker admonished. "That is playground behavior, and you are in the house."

"Yes, ma'am." He froze in place. "Can we go, Daddy? Can we go to the cabin?"

"Yes, Jonathan. Mr. Everett said he would go up and check on the cabin tomorrow and do any repairs, and Mrs. Everett will clean it up and stock the pantry. Everything will be ready by Wednesday." He turned to Mrs. Tucker. "Mrs. Tucker, you will have several extra days off, with pay of course. We'll leave Wednesday and stay through the weekend."

"Be ready first thing Wednesday morning," he said to Marnie. "We'll leave right after breakfast."

Chapter 32

The drive up into the mountains was beautiful. Trees that had been bare were showing the first signs of green on the tips of their branches, contrasting with the dark green of the conifers. The mountains in the far distance had snow on their peaks, and David explained that it would remain through most of the summer. When they rounded a curve in the road, a verdant valley unfolded before them, and they could see deer grazing in the distance.

There were times, though, when Marnie was nervous, especially when they were meeting other vehicles. Her fingers would tighten around the armrest on the door, and she realized she was holding her breath until there was no other car nearby.

"Are you OK?" he asked once.

"Um . . . yes," she replied.

After nearly two hours of driving, David pulled into a small service station. "Almost there," he announced. "Let's go check in with the Evertons." Marnie and Jonathan piled out of the car and followed him into the store.

"Well, look who's here," said the gray-haired man. "Dina, come see this young man who's come to visit." He came out from behind the counter and stood in front of Jonathan. "I figure you must have grown a foot since we saw you last fall, Jonathan. Pretty soon you'll be as tall as me." He turned to David and stuck out his hand. "David, it's good to see you again." He nodded in Marnie's direction. "Mrs. Barrett."

A pleasant-looking woman came from the back of the store, feather duster in hand and a smile on her face. "David, you're looking well." Her smile grew when she spotted Jonathan. "Chad, I think you're right. This boy is going to be taller than either you or David."

Jonathan giggled under all the attention and clung to Marnie's leg. The older woman's greeting to Marnie was almost as brief as her husband's. "Mrs. Barrett, good to see you again."

Neither Chad nor Dina Everett had been rude, but it was plain they were not as happy to see Marnie as they were David and Jonathan. Marnie wondered if she had done something to offend them or if they didn't like her because of her reputation.

"Everything's tip-top up at the cabin," Chad said. "No winter damage that I could see. I fired up the generator, so you'll have lights and heat. There's a good stack of firewood on the front porch. I imagine you'll be wanting a fire in the evenings. And there's plenty of gas to keep the generator going."

"I dusted and ran a mop around, so it's pretty clean." Dina said. "I wiped out the refrigerator and stocked it with milk and juice and some other things. There's a supply of canned goods in the pantry—enough for a few days anyway"—she ruffled Jonathan's hair—"and I left some cookies I thought this young man would like."

"I thank you both," David said as he pulled out his wallet, "for keeping watch over the place and for starting it up in the spring." He tossed several bills onto the counter. "I couldn't rest easy about the cabin if I didn't have you two here taking care of it for me."

They said their goodbyes and drove another mile along the highway then turned onto a graveled side road. After another half mile, they turned onto a dirt track leading slightly uphill for another half mile or so. Rounding a curve, Marnie caught sight of a log cabin nestled in a stand of evergreens. To the right and slightly downhill was a blue lake glistening in the sunshine, with a winding path leading to it.

"Oh, David! It looks like something you'd see on a postcard."

"You like it?" he questioned.

"It's beautiful, simply beautiful," she replied.

"Let's get unloaded," he said, and they each carried something into the cabin.

Marnie took a moment to fix the house in her memory. It was built of logs and had a bright green metal roof. Three steps led to a covered porch that extended across the front.

David pulled a key from his jacket pocket and unlocked the front door. They stepped into a great room with log walls and wide plank wood floors covered with oriental rugs, soft and muted with age. A woodsy scent filled the air. A massive stone fireplace filled the majority of one wall, while a kitchen took up the back left corner of the room. Leather couches and chairs had brightly colored quilts and Native American patterned rugs thrown casually across their backs, ready for use if the air was chilly. Vibrant, abstract paintings dotted the walls where Marnie would have expected typical landscape paintings.

"This is the most comfortable room I've ever seen," Marnie exclaimed.

"Really? How do you know?" David said, grinning.

"I just know," she replied. "It's perfect. I love it!"

"I like it better than our house," Jonathan said.

"I know," David said, and Marnie wondered if he might add, "I do too."

David led the way to a door on the back wall that led to a short hall where two small bedrooms were separated by a bathroom. One bedroom had a queen-sized bed, and the other held two twin beds.

"Jonathan and I will bunk in here," David said as he slung his duffle bag onto one of the beds. "You can have the other room."

By the time they had their bags in their rooms, Jonathan was ready to go to the dock. "We're not quite ready yet,

Sport. Mrs. Grady sent a cooler full of food, and we need to unload that and eat some lunch first."

They all trooped back to the SUV to unload the rest of the cargo. In the cooler, they found all sorts of prepared food, including sandwiches for lunch, along with carrot and celery sticks, fruit juice, and cookies. There was a casserole ready to pop into the oven for supper, complete with baking instructions from Mrs. Grady and a loaf of garlic bread.

"Everyone's making sure you have plenty of cookies," Marnie remarked.

"Yum," Jonathan replied.

After lunch they took the path down to the dock that stretched a short way out over the water. The lake wasn't large, only about twenty acres. In the summertime, they had access to a flat-bottomed boat. For now, though, they would just admire it from the shore. Jonathan wanted to go fishing, but David nixed that idea.

"We didn't buy any bait, son, and the ground is still too cold to dig for worms. They're still down deep so they don't freeze. Maybe next time we come we can fish. The fish will be down deep in the water now, too."

"So they don't freeze, too?" Jonathan asked.

"That's right," his father answered. "But I'll tell you what, we can play Go Fish with cards."

"Hurray!" Jonathan cheered then sobered. "Can't we stay down here for a while?"

"Sure. Want to skip rocks?" David asked as he bent over to search out a stone.

Immediately caught up in the idea, Jonathan started looking for a rock of his own. Marnie went and sat on the dock, dangled her feet over the edge and admired the vista before her.

I don't remember when I've felt so peaceful, she thought and then laughed at herself for such a silly idea. *Duh,* she almost said out loud.

The sun had begun to sink behind the mountains in the west, and the air began to cool when David suggested they go back to the cabin. Jonathan led the way, although David cautioned him to stay with them. "Surely he can go on ahead," Marnie commented. "It's only a short way, and we can see all the way to the cabin."

David said nothing, but when they reached the house and Jonathan bounded up the steps and through the front door, he put his hand on Marnie's arm, holding her back. "I didn't want to say anything in front of Jonathan, but sometimes there are bears in this area . . ."

"Bears?" Marnie yelped.

"Shh. When I talked to Chad on the phone Monday he said there haven't been any spotted around here this spring, but it's always a good idea to keep Jonathan close to us, just in case."

Marnie glanced nervously around them as if she might see a bear amble up at any time.

"What should we do if we see one?" she asked.

"First of all, stay calm. Don't panic. If the bear is on the path, you move off it. Speak in a moderate tone of voice. You should talk so the bear knows you're a human, not another animal, but you shouldn't scream or yell at it. Don't look it in the eye, and back up slowly until you are a good distance away from it. Don't ever run. Bears will chase you if you run."

"If I meet a bear, I'll probably just faint, and then it will eat me," she said.

"We probably won't see one, even from a distance, but I don't want Jonathan getting away from us, just to be safe."

"Agreed. I'm not getting a distance away from you, either."

David was chuckling when they entered the cabin.

Marnie put the casserole in the oven for supper, and she, David, and Jonathan played several wild hands of Go Fish with a deck of cards David took from an oversized antique armoire in the living room. When the timer went off, David and Jonathan washed up and then set the table while Marnie put the bread in the oven. A few minutes later they sat down to supper.

It was a quiet meal, and when it was over, Marnie said, "Jonathan, I think you'd better go take your bath before you fall asleep. It's been a busy day, and I can tell you're tired."

"Aww," he began, but David cut him off.

"I'll come draw a tub of water for you and help you get started."

"Be sure he washes all over instead of just playing in the tub," Marnie advised.

By the time she had cleared the table and washed the dishes, David had Jonathan bathed and in his pajamas. Together they tucked the yawning boy into one of the twin beds.

"Leave the lamp on, please Daddy, until you come to bed," he requested.

"Sure thing, Sport. I'll turn it off later."

Marnie pulled the covers up around Jonathan's shoulders and kissed him on the forehead.

"Good night, sweet one," she whispered.

Chapter 33

When they returned to the living room, David went to the fireplace. Chad had prepared everything for lighting a fire. Kindling and starter twigs and cones filled the opening, and logs sat on the massive stone hearth. David took a butane starter from the mantle and lit the dry sticks. When they were enveloped in flames, he added small pieces of wood, and as the fire grew, he added larger logs. When it was burning to his satisfaction, he joined Marnie on the sofa.

They sat in silence and watched the flames.

Marnie broke the silence. "I imagine if it weren't for having to earn a living a person could live up here. It's so peaceful."

David turned his body squarely toward her.

"What's the matter?" she asked. "Did I say something wrong?"

He shook his head. "Marnie, like many of the places I've taken you since you returned home, this trip had a purpose, too. At first, I'll admit, when I took you someplace, like the Roadhouse, I thought I'd catch you in a lie—catch you pretending to have amnesia." He rose and used the poker to push the burning log to the back of the pile and added a new piece of wood to the front.

"After I became convinced you weren't making the whole thing up, I did it to try to spark a memory. Sort of like when you drove to the mall and parked in the same spot you did when you ran off with Ray. Your subconscious did that, but it didn't take you any further.

"Nothing seemed to work. No more memories came through. Then I thought about bringing you up here. You and I came up here not long after Jonathan was born. You were so stressed out over having a baby, so sure you couldn't take care of an infant, you didn't even want to try. My mother found Mrs. Tucker to take care of Jonathan. She had been working for another family in Mother's circle until the children got too old to need her. I brought you up here to calm you down, to try to talk to you and get our marriage to work."

"I don't remember anything about being up here before. Did I like it?"

"No. You disliked it intensely. Being out here 'in the wilds,' as you called it, made you even more upset. You hated it, and after a couple of days, you threw a fit, and I took you back to town."

Marnie could only stare in dismay. She turned back and fixed her gaze on the flames.

"I've been thinking a lot about what might have happened to me."

"So have I."

"I think it might have been a car wreck."

"Why do you say that?" he asked.

"Driving up here today, I got very nervous several times. Meeting big trucks, especially, made me panicky. Was there anything before, any reason you know of, that a situation like that might scare me?"

"No. To my knowledge you've never been in a wreck of any kind."

"Driving around town hasn't bothered me at all, but it was all I could do to keep from screaming when we met a big truck on the road up here."

David seemed perplexed. "But you didn't have any bruises or scrapes on your body."

Marnie sighed. "I know. So that doesn't really fit, does it? But still, that's what I feel."

They continued to reflect on that idea.

"I think whatever happened to me must have scared me

so much I decided I didn't want to live my life the way I had been. From what you tell me, I'm different than I used to be."

"Yes, you are. You are definitely changed in many ways, but you're still you, if you know what I mean."

"I'm not sure that I do."

"I've been doing a lot of thinking lately, too, about what you were like when we first met, what you were like during our marriage, and the difference in what you're like now. When we first hooked up, you were sassy and sexy and made no bones about wanting to be in my bed. Yes, you deliberately got pregnant in order to trap me into marriage. But on the other hand, there was a side of you then that I see now. You listened to my sorrows and troubles, my doubts about myself, and you were kind and comforting. That's the side I see in you now. That's the side I fell in love with—the side I kept thinking about when we married."

"I'm glad to hear not everything about me was bad. It sounds like even though I was determined to get you to marry me, I was at least somewhat nice to you," Marnie said. "I must have at least liked you, if not loved you."

"Yes, you were. And you did have a good side. I wouldn't have fallen for you if you hadn't—wouldn't have married you. I realized I didn't really have to marry you. If I truly didn't want to, you couldn't make me. But I saw the kind side of you, too, the side that listened and cared and encouraged me. I kept thinking that side of you would shine through once we were married and you didn't have to worry about catching me anymore.

"But"—he paused and took a deep breath—"I was wrong. You became more concerned about parties and clothes and friends that I didn't want to have anything to do with. I kept hoping you'd show me the sweet part of you again, but you didn't . . . until you disappeared and came back. Now the part of you I fell in love with is back even stronger. It's like you were a kid, a teenager, and now you've grown up and settled down. Whatever happened to you matured you, that's for sure."

Marnie wondered if David was telling her he still loved her, telling her there was still a chance their marriage might work.

"Oh, you're still sexy as hell, but you don't have to flaunt it like you used to. Looking back, it was almost like you thought no one would notice you, no one would like you, if you didn't wear provocative clothes. You're surer of yourself now—not out to prove anything."

"Sure of myself? I'm about as unsure of myself as anyone who can't remember their past can be."

"Oh, you're surer than you think. You've said to me several times you know who you are deep down inside, and you aren't the woman who wore the clothes in your closet. That's why you got rid of them. Whatever happened to you has made you look into your psyche to find the Marnie you are determined to be from now on."

"I hope so. What worries me more than anything is when the memories come flooding back I'll turn back into the hedonistic Marnie."

"I just don't see that happening. At least I hope not."

"I hope not, too," she muttered.

Chapter 34

The fire crackled and popped as Marnie thought about all that had been said and wondered about both the past and the future. She gazed into the yellow and orange hues of the flames, imagining pictures in the fire, hoping it would stir some memory of the last time she had been there with David.

David rose and went to put another log on the fire. He adjusted the logs with the poker and stood in front of the flames, absorbing their warmth.

"I'll admit there isn't much to do up here. There's no TV to watch, for example."

"You know, I hadn't even missed it."

"The only reception up here is by satellite, and it isn't worth it to pay for service we seldom use."

"If we come up here often, it might be a good idea to bring a TV and a DVD player. We could watch movies, and it might be good entertainment for Jonathan if we have a rainy day and he can't go outside."

"You're right. That's a good idea. He does like to play with his cars out on the porch if it's rainy, but sometimes when a front moves through, it's too cold."

After a couple of minutes, Marnie spoke. "Could I ask you something about this whole business?"

"Sure. Ask away."

"Can you tell me about the project Ray stole? You said its loss endangered the future of Barrett's. Is that true? What happens if you never find Ray and the . . . thing, whatever it is?"

"I can't be more specific about what it is. That's a military secret. I have several people trying to recreate the project to the point it was at when Ray took off with the prototype and plans. Even if we are able to reproduce the whole project, it'll put us way behind schedule, and the government won't be happy about that. I have a meeting with government officials in about six weeks, and they're expecting to see what I had before Ray absconded with it. Ray is probably trying to sell it to a competitor. Whether another company will buy it and take the risk of being accused of stealing it or of corporate espionage, I don't know. I have six weeks left to do something."

"Well, I hope you find Ray and get your work back, unharmed and unsold. I'm so ashamed I was part of anything like that. I know apologies won't help, but I am sorry. Even if I didn't help steal it, I was part of the escape, and for that I apologize."

"Let's just let it drop for tonight. I brought us up here to get away from all of that. Even if being here didn't bring back any memories, we can relax and forget that particular pressure for a couple of days."

"OK. That's fine with me."

"We do have a few entertainments here in the wilds," he said, as he moved toward the armoire. Marnie followed. He opened the doors, and she saw a shelf full of books. Scanning the titles, she found war stories and mysteries, left by the men who had traveled to the cabin in years past.

"Some of these mysteries might be good," she said. She noticed a stack of magazines and picked one off the pile. It was a fashion magazine from four years ago, and the one under it was a tabloid with movie stars' pictures scattered across the front.

"You left those magazines that one time you came," David explained. "Dina never throws anything out when she cleans up after we leave."

"Well, I'll throw them out." Marnie gathered the magazines and threw them in the trashcan when she walked into the kitchen. As she turned to return to the living room, a scratching noise came from the armoire.

"We do have this radio to provide some entertainment. If we're lucky, we might pick up a station. Reception is so bad up here in the mountains we don't even have cell phone service except in certain places, and this cabin isn't one of them."

He adjusted the dial on the set, trying to get a clear signal. At last, the sound of music drifted into the room. Violins uttered sweet tones, and a trumpet echoed the melody as an orchestra offered songs from decades past. David held out his hand.

"Would you care to dance?" he asked.

It seemed automatic for Marnie to place her hand in his. "I don't know if I know how to dance," she said as he placed her hand on his shoulder and took her other hand in his.

"For sure you know how to fast dance," David replied as he pulled her closer and started moving to the music.

"I do . . . did?"

"You did. You could dirty dance until every man within eyesight got a . . . er . . . was visibly aroused, if you get my meaning . . . when you were on the dance floor."

Marnie was so embarrassed she tried to pull away from her husband's grasp, but his hand on her back kept her close.

"Uh-uh. Don't pull away. To answer your question, I don't know if you slow dance or not. I don't recall us ever dancing this way. They don't play music like this at the Roadhouse, but you shouldn't have any trouble with it."

He moved her slightly away from him and looked down at their feet. "See, this way," he said. "Step, slide, step. Then back again, step, slide, step." They practiced a few steps. He then pulled her back close to him again.

"See, it's coming back to you," he said. "Just feel my hand on your back guiding you."

It felt right to Marnie to be in his arms, like coming home. She let her cheek rest on his shoulder and closed her eyes, drifting along with the music. She felt him lay his cheek on the top of her head, and he pulled her even closer. Their bodies fit together like two parts of a puzzle, interconnected to make a perfect picture. *But a picture of what?* she wondered.

David released her right hand, and removing his hand from her back, he urged both of her hands up beyond his shoulders. Her arms encircled his neck as his wrapped around her body. One of his hands urged her even closer, pulling her against the hardness of his erection. His lips found the soft skin beneath her ear, kissing ever lower. When he started to set her away from him, she was so dizzy with arousal she almost fell. She moaned in disappointment, sure he was going to end the encounter.

"Shh," he whispered. "It's OK. It's not over." He reached for the radio and turned it off. Putting one arm around her, he pulled her toward him and kissed her, his tongue briefly outlining her lips. He broke the kiss to guide her toward the bedroom. "It's just beginning."

Chapter 35

Something aroused Marnie from her sleep, and she snuggled more closely to David's back. The bare skin of her breasts and stomach found his warm skin comforting. She was drifting back into slumber when a noise brought her back.

"Daddy . . . Daddy," a small voice whispered.

"Mmm."

"Daddy."

"Jonathan?" David said sleepily.

"Daddy, you said you were going to sleep in the other bed. When I woke up you weren't there."

"It's OK, Jonathan. I decided to sleep here instead," David's sleepy voice explained.

"You weren't there, Daddy, and I was scared. I looked for you, and you weren't in the living room or kitchen. I didn't know where you were."

"I'm sorry I didn't tell you, Sport. But it's OK now." David patted his son on the arm. "Tell you what. Go get dressed. Get a clean pair of jeans and a clean shirt and put them on. I'll meet you in the kitchen in a few minutes."

"OK, Daddy." Jonathan left the room, pulling door shut behind him.

David rolled over to face Marnie, and she pulled the covers up over her bare breasts.

"Busted," he said with a grin and kissed her on the nose. "Good morning."

"Good morning," she replied, a wide smile on her face.

"I told myself this wouldn't happen, but somehow

you've worked your way into my heart again." He brushed her hair back from her face.

Marnie stared into his eyes. "And you are in mine. Even though I don't remember you from before, you are somewhere deep in my heart and mind. My soul remembers you."

"No matter how I fight it, the passion between us pulls me in and my common sense flies out the window." He kissed her long and hard then pulled back. "I'd love to spend the day right here with you, but I guess I'd better go see to our son before he comes back." He rose and slipped into the jeans he had discarded on the floor the night before. Picking up his shirt and shoes, he smiled at her and left the room. A minute later, she heard the water running in the bathroom.

Marnie rose and retrieved her robe from the suitcase, putting it on before the chill of the room could sink in or Jonathan came back. She laid out her clothes for the day, a pair of jeans and the pink sweatshirt she had worn her first day out of bed after her illness.

David stuck his head into the room. "Bathroom's all yours!"

Marnie gathered her bathing gear and went to take a shower, needing to remove the scent of lovemaking that enveloped her. When she entered the kitchen a few minutes later, she found David frying bacon and Jonathan on a stool at the bar that separated the kitchen from the living room. He was busy at work.

"I'm making the toast for breakfast," he declared proudly.

"Just have a seat. It'll be ready in a minute," David said.

"Why don't I pour the juice?" she suggested and started toward the cabinet holding the glasses.

"OK. Your men were going to fix breakfast for you, but if you insist," David joked.

"Yeah, your men were fixing your breakfast," Jonathan intoned as he took two slices from the toaster.

David reached over and kissed her lightly on the lips as

she passed by him then turned to Jonathan. "I think that's enough toast, buddy. If we need more later, I'll let you fix it."

After they had eaten, David started gathering the dirty dishes from the table.

"If you two can handle the cleanup, I'm going to go take a shower," he said.

"Can we handle the cleanup?" Marnie asked Jonathan.

"Sure," he said.

David returned in jeans and a plaid flannel shirt just as Marnie dried the last plate and put it away.

"What shall we do today?" His question was directed to Jonathan, but as he spoke, he came up behind Marnie and put his arms around her, burying his face into her shoulder and giving her a kiss on the neck. She shivered and leaned her head back against him.

"Later," he whispered.

Jonathan was bouncing up and down on his toes. "Let's go back to the lake!"

"That sounds good to me, but let me get something first." He went to the armoire and rummaged through one of the bottom drawers.

"Aha!" he said and pulled out two sets of binoculars. He handed one pair to Marnie and put the strap of the other around his neck.

"What are those, Daddy?"

"Binoculars," he replied. "They help you see a long way off. I'll show you how to use them when we get to the lake."

A few minutes later they reached the dock, and David had them sit in the middle of it.

"Why can't we sit on the edge?" Jonathan asked. "I like to hang my legs off."

"Sometime we can do that, but I need to watch to be sure you don't fall off. I can't do that and use the binoculars at the same time. I want to teach you how to use them, too."

"I won't fall off!"

"I want to be sure of that. You might get so interested in what you're seeing that you make a mistake. And it's still much too cool to be swimming in the lake. Middle of the dock, Sport."

David and Marnie viewed their surroundings through the lenses.

"When can I look?" Jonathan whined.

"Let me find something for you to look at," David replied. "Oh. OK, now, here," he said as he situated Jonathan's hands on the binoculars and brought them up to his face. He turned the boy's head slightly. "See? Right over there across the lake? It's a deer with her baby. See it?"

It took a minute for Jonathan to zoom in on the shy creatures, but once he did he was enthralled. "The momma's getting a drink, Daddy! She's drinking out of the lake."

Marnie was watching the deer also and said to Jonathan, "The mother deer is called a doe, and the baby deer is called a fawn."

"Marnie, may I use your binoculars for a minute?"

She handed them over and shortly afterward David remarked, "I thought so." He handed them back to her. "Look in the trees behind them. See the buck standing guard?" He helped Jonathan move his sight slightly. "Look there, Jonathan. The buck, the daddy deer, is in the trees behind them."

"Oh, Daddy. I see him. It's a whole deer family. Momma, daddy, and little boy, just like us."

Marnie and David looked at each other. Behind Jonathan, David clasped her hand.

"Yes, son. A family, just like us."

Chapter 36

They spent the morning on the dock observing the wildlife. After the deer family melded back into the forest, Marnie spotted a mother duck with a string of ducklings trailing behind her. They popped in and out among the reeds some distance down the shore. The binoculars made them seem as if they were within arm's reach.

"Is there a daddy duck?" Jonathan wanted to know.

"Yes," David answered. "There's a daddy duck somewhere. He's just not with them right now."

"Maybe he had to go to work," Jonathan surmised.

"Maybe."

In a clearing not far away, a rabbit appeared to be eating the new shoots of grass that were thriving because of the spring weather. Occasionally, it would sit up and look around, nose twitching, alert for any danger that might be coming its way.

Finally, Jonathan became bored with the surroundings.

"Can we go skip rocks?"

David and Jonathan skipped rocks across the water, David's skipping two or three times, Jonathan's sinking immediately. Marnie stayed on the dock, occasionally lifting the binoculars to observe what might be foraging for food on the bank across the way.

"We're hungry," David called. "We men are ready for lunch."

"Yeah, we men are ready for lunch," came his little echo.

After a break for sandwiches, Marnie asked Jonathan what he wanted to do next.

"I want to play in the dirt!"

His answer surprised her, but after she thought about it, she realized he had no chance to do what most boys his age did—to play outside in the dirt, to dig and not worry about what an adult was going to say. The women in his life before now—Ruth and Mrs. Tucker—weren't likely to let him do that, and Marnie herself hadn't been a part of his activities.

David pulled two rocking chairs from the living room onto the front porch, and Jonathan settled himself in the yard directly in front of them. He used twigs and rocks to build streets for his toy cars, arranging them over and over.

"He did this last fall when I brought him up here," David said.

"Did I come?"

"No. You said you had enough of the place the one time you had been here."

Marnie sighed and leaned her head back against the chair.

"When I saw the rug with the city streets on it you bought him, I thought he must have told you about playing this way in the dirt. It's sort of a fancy and cleaner way of playing the same thing."

"If he did, I don't remember it. I just picked out something I thought he'd like."

"And he does. I feel guilty for not noticing he didn't have many toys appropriate for his age. On the weekends we usually go play somewhere, but I hadn't thought to shop for him."

They sat silently, rocking in their chairs, while they watched Jonathan. Finally, David spoke. "I wish the sun would hurry and go down."

She looked at him curiously. "Why?"

"So it would be time to go to bed."

Marnie was sure she blushed at the statement, but she felt the same way.

They could hear the sound of an approaching vehicle in the distance. "Jonathan, someone's coming. Come up here on the porch."

Jonathan snatched up a couple of cars and mounted the steps.

When a green pickup truck rounded the last turn, David said, "That's Chad Everett. I wonder what's up."

The older man parked beside David's SUV, got out, and approached the cabin.

"You folks look like you're enjoying the day," he said as he walked toward them.

"We are that," David replied. "What brings you out here?"

"You have a phone call. Your mother called and asked me to have you call home. She said it 'might be important' but wasn't an emergency. That's what she said, 'might be important.'"

"Thanks for driving out here to tell me, Chad. I'll be to the store shortly to call her."

They watched Chad get in his truck, circle the area, and leave.

"Do you want to come with me or stay here?" he asked Marnie.

"Let's go, too," Jonathan begged. "Please?"

"Do you want us to stay here?" she asked.

"No. It's fine to go with me. Jonathan," he said, turning to his dust-covered son, "brush as much of that dust off as possible and then go in and wash up."

"I'd better go and use a washcloth on him," Marnie said.

When they were in the vehicle headed toward the country store, Marnie said, "I wonder what might be important but isn't an emergency?"

"I'm hoping it has something to do with finding Ray," David said tersely.

"Can you use your cell phone when we get to the store?"

"Not likely. Even when I can get through from there, I usually end up with a dropped call. I'll use the Everett's phone."

When they arrived at the store, Dina said, "David, you go on back in the office and use the phone there. It'll give you some privacy."

"Jonathan and I will get a couple of sodas and sit out front to wait for you," Marnie told him.

They went to the cooler where Jonathan picked out an orange drink.

"That looks good, Jonathan. I think I'll get one, too."

She went to the counter to pay, and Dina, a little friendlier than she had been earlier commented, "You're lucky to get a seat on the bench today. Usually old Mr. Gretchem and his buddy Silas Moore sit out there and watch the cars go by, but Silas went to Boulder to visit his daughter and Mr. Gretchem's arthritis is acting up, so he stayed home."

Marnie and Jonathan were sitting on the long wooden bench, drinking their orange sodas and watching the cars go by, when David returned. He sat down beside Marnie, sighed, and looked off into the distance.

"So what is it? Did someone find Ray?"

"No. It didn't have anything to do with Ray," he answered.

He turned toward her with a serious look on his face. "Marnie, I know you can't remember anything, but there are some coincidences happening, some things leading us toward Phoenix."

"Like me recognizing the Suns on TV?"

"Yes, like that. My mother said there was a phone call this morning from a detective with the Phoenix Police Department. He wouldn't tell her what was going on, but she assumed it might have something to do with Ray, so she called me. The detective wanted to talk to you, not me, and left a number for you to call.

"At this point in the story, I still assumed it had something to do with Ray. Maybe he was in jail there or something."

"Should I call and find out?"

"I took it upon myself to call for you. I explained to the detective that you are my wife and have been ill and suffering from amnesia. I told him you really couldn't remember much of your past, only a few odd moments that didn't amount to much."

"So, did he tell you what's going on?"

"Yes, yes he did. It seems as if a woman in Phoenix has disappeared. Her name is Martha Kelley. Her landlady reported her missing. She's been gone for weeks, but the landlady thought she was traveling for her job. When she found out the woman wasn't working, she called the police and reported her missing. The police went through the apartment and found a slip of paper with your name and cell phone number on it. When they couldn't get anywhere with the cell number, they traced it. The cell phone company gave them your contact information. They want to know what you know about it."

"My goodness," Marnie breathed. "Somebody in Phoenix was calling me? I wonder what for."

"The only thing that comes to mind is maybe Ray dumped you and took off with someone else and that woman was calling you for some reason."

"If only I could remember," Marnie said, needlessly. "But her name, it sounds familiar, like I ought to know her."

"There's only one thing we can do," David said. "We're going to Phoenix. I told the detective we'd be there tomorrow."

Chapter 37

"Detective Mendez? I'm David Barrett. My wife and I flew into Phoenix last night and checked into a hotel. I decided I want to find out more about the missing woman . . . Martha Kelley."

Marnie paced the floor as she listened to David's conversation with the police detective he had spoken with the day before. She had been on edge ever since they landed the night before. After speaking to the detective in charge of the investigation, they had rushed back to the cabin, packed, and drove back home. When they reached an area where there was clear cell phone reception, David called his secretary and had her make reservations on an evening flight to Phoenix and book a hotel room.

Marnie was fine until they landed, when it seemed as if a buzzing started in her brain and wouldn't stop. Scents and sounds threatened to overwhelm her as she tried to take in everything around her. When they deplaned and reached the concourse, she turned to the left without thinking, and David grabbed her by the arm.

"Let me see which way we go to get out of here," he said, glancing at the signs.

"It's this way," she answered confidently.

"You're sure?"

"Yes, I'm sure."

"Then you must have flow here before," he replied.

"I guess I must have. I think I know my way around here," she said, standing there in the flow of people headed this way or that, "and this is the way to go to get out."

Sky Harbor Airport felt like home to her, like she had been there many times. That's when the energy started buzzing through her, like she had a jillion things to do and keep track of, except she couldn't think of a single one of them now. It made her nervous, and she wondered if her memories were going to come bursting back with no warning. She held on to David's arm as they made their way to the rental car booths.

Later that night, as they were falling asleep, Marnie told David about the feelings she had been having. "Do you suppose I flew into Phoenix with Ray and that's why the airport seemed familiar?"

"I know Ray flew out in his small plane, but he could have flown it to any major city, then you two could have taken a commercial flight to Phoenix. That would have been a good way to throw us off the trail. Ray's plane hasn't been located anywhere, so I'd say it's a distinct possibility you did just that."

Marnie was replaying the scene at the airport in her head as she listened to David. She hoped if she went over it enough times something would click and she'd remember any other time she had gotten off a plane there.

"Yesterday when we talked, I told you I'd get back to you. Let me tell you why I'm so interested, Detective Mendez. An employee of mine, Ray Boling, stole something from my company—company secrets, you might say—and disappeared. There have been signs he might be trying to sell those secrets to a firm here in Phoenix. I'd like to find out if this Martha Kelley is involved some way. Maybe she is with him . . . I don't know. It's important that I find Ray Boling and get my property back before he sells it to one of my competitors." He paused as he listened to the man on the other end of the connection.

"I'm afraid I can't tell you that. It's top secret . . . involved with the government."

As she listened to the conversation, Marnie watched the city out the window and tried to put together the jigsaw of clues and make sense of what was happening.

"Maybe this Ms. Kelley was a go-between for Boling and a buyer. That's what I want to find out." David's voice was growing impatient. "Uh-huh. Yes." He listened for a minute without speaking. "You say there *were* signs of a struggle? Uh-huh."

Marnie's anxiety increased when she heard violence was involved, and she began pacing as she trembled with apprehension.

"No, I have no idea why Ms. Kelley would be calling my wife. Neither she nor I know Ms. Kelley. The name doesn't ring a bell. Would it be possible for my wife and me to see the place where you found the paper with her name and phone number on it? Perhaps there is something else there I might recognize as having significance to the matter. Yes . . . yes, I have a pad and pen . . . go ahead." David scribbled an address.

"I've got it. I'd like to meet with this landlady. I have a picture of Boling, and I'd like to see if she recognizes him . . . if she's seen him with Ms. Kelley."

When David got off the phone, he turned to Marnie. "Come sit down, and I'll tell you what I found out."

She was shaking so hard when she sat down across the small table from him that he moved his chair closer to her and grasped her hands in his.

"Shh. It's going to be OK." He tried to soothe her, but it did no good. "Why are you so upset? Are things coming back to you?"

"Maybe. There's something . . . I don't know what. Oh, David, I'm so frightened!"

"What of?"

"That's just it, I don't know," she squeezed his hands and held tight. "David, you told the detective you have a picture of Ray Boling. I don't remember his name, but maybe seeing his picture would bring something back to me."

David reached into the open briefcase sitting on the table and drew out an employment form with a picture of a square-jawed, sandy-haired man, in his late thirties, and placed it in front of Marnie.

She immediately cried out and shrank back against the chair.

"You recognize him?" David said, excitedly. "I don't know why I didn't show you a picture before. That's what you needed to start your memory working again!"

"David, he's evil! I don't remember anything except I'm so scared of him. He made me . . . he made me . . ."

"What? What did he make you do?"

"I don't remember, David," she held her hands up to her spinning head. "I still don't remember! I just know he wanted me to do something, and I was frightened and didn't want to do it."

"Calm down, sweetheart. Calm down. It's coming back to you," he said in a composed voice. "Don't be upset. It's all working out now. It'll be OK."

"But, David, you said there were signs of a struggle, and now she's missing. What if . . . what if Ray . . . killed her? What if I'm involved in a murder? What if that's the trauma that made me lose my memory?"

Chapter 38

David held her close, his arms sheltering her and his strong hands rubbing her back. His voice was deep and calm as he tried to alleviate her fears.

"Whatever it is, I'll be there with you, but I can't imagine any circumstances in which you or Ray would kill someone. He's a jerk, all right, and a thief, but not a murderer. And neither are you." His hand touched her hair, brushing it back from her face. "Yes, you've done some irresponsible things, and you've been thoughtless about other people's feelings, but that's a long way from murder. Don't let your imagination paint pictures that never happened."

Marnie drew back in the circle of his arms so she could see his face as she spoke. "But the detective said there were signs of violence, right? Something bad had to have happened. And seeing the picture of Ray, I know something happened in connection with him, something that made me frightened of him. I can't remember what it was, I can't even remember *him*, but I was frightened when I saw his face."

"The detective said there was no blood," David said, "no sign anyone was injured, just a small table turned over, a lamp and some papers on the floor, things like that. Let's not make more of it than it is. Detective Mendez said they are investigating it, but that there is nothing to make them believe Martha Kelley is dead. She may have had a fight with a boyfriend. On the other hand, she may have gone out of town with a friend—male or female." David released her from his arms and stepped away. He reached for one of her hands, drawing her toward the bed.

"Ray is out for number one, himself, and his main objective at this point is to sell the plans and prototype for a lot of money." David sat down on the side of the bed and urged her down beside him. "He wouldn't have done anything to jeopardize his chances for a big payoff. So that pretty much eliminates the chance he hurt or killed someone. He just wants to get away with the money without being caught, and committing assault or murder wouldn't fit in those plans. Besides, I've always thought of Ray as a coward at heart. That's why I don't understand your being afraid of him. You've known him for a long time, even if you don't remember it. If you were frightened of him, you would never have left town with him."

David's words comforted Marnie. "I guess you're right. I don't know why I reacted so strongly. I think this whole memory loss thing is wearing on my nerves more than I thought."

"Losing your past would be harrowing on anyone. You have a right to be nervous and upset."

Marnie nodded her head in agreement, but she was determined to get ahold of her emotions. Nothing could be gained by losing control.

"Let me call the landlady and see if we can meet with her." David retrieved his cell phone from the table. "Maybe she can shed some light on this puzzle."

David called the phone number he had gotten from Detective Mendez and introduced himself as the husband of the woman whose name and phone number were found in Ms. Kelley's apartment. He asked her if they could meet and try to figure out what happened and how his wife was involved.

"Part of the problem, Mrs. Oberle, is that my wife recently suffered a severe trauma which left her with amnesia. She can't remember anything that happened before a few weeks ago. We hope that if we can figure out what connection she has with Ms. Kelley and why Ms. Kelley called her, it will help bring back my wife's memory. If it does, maybe we'll know where Ms. Kelley went," he explained, trying to simplify the complicated story.

He wrote an address on the pad of paper. "We'll be there within the hour. Thank you for seeing us."

The GPS in the rental car helped them easily find the address. The neighborhood was a modest one, filled with single-family homes. The front yards were mostly neatly raked sand or gravel. A few homeowners had obviously tried to maintain a small grass expanse, but in Phoenix's climate, they had little success. Although yucca and cactus were the plants of choice, a few yards boasted small trees that gave minimal shade.

Marnie watched closely as they drove through the city. As they neared their destination, she felt more certain she had been there before. The buildings along the streets they traveled resonated within her, as if she had seen them in the past. The houses were built of various materials and sat on small lots. Some were stucco, some wood, and some covered with siding. The neighborhood was older, but the area was clean and well kept.

The closer they came to the Oberle home, the tighter Marnie's nerves seemed to be stretched. Her heart was pounding so strongly it felt as if it would jump out of her chest. She knew without a doubt they were coming to the center of the mystery of her lost memory, and although she wanted her memory back and this uncertainty to be over, she was nervous and afraid of what she might find out.

They pulled up in front of a stucco house, terra cotta in color. A long covered porch extended the full breadth of the home, which was larger than the other houses on the block. The yard was neat and clean, covered with small gravel. A fairly large tree shaded a good deal of area, and large blue pots sat on either side of the single step.

Marnie looked at the house, and her head started spinning. "This looks familiar," she told David. "I've been here before. I know I have."

They remained in the car while Marnie looked at the house and David watched Marnie. He finally spoke. "Anything else? Just that it looks familiar?"

She shook her head. "No, that's all for now. But my head is swimming. Something else is coming."

David went around and opened the car door. Marnie slid out; she had to cling to his arm to keep from stumbling. The whole world seemed to be revolving, as if she were in the center of a top that was spinning around her. With great effort, she cleared her vision and walked beside David to the porch. When they stepped into the shady space, they noticed two front doors, both painted cerulean blue—bright and welcoming. David guided her toward the nearest one.

Above an old-fashioned doorbell button was a small piece of paper that read "R. Oberle." David pushed the button then placed his hand over Marnie's. She gripped his hand, trying to gather what reassurance she could from his touch. The things they were about to learn might devastate her, and no matter how unsettled their relationship was, he was her only hold to reality, however tenuous that might be.

The woman who opened the door appeared to be in her fifties: gray-headed and plump, she looked like a picture of a perfect grandmother.

Her eyes went to David as he introduced himself. "Mrs. Oberle, I'm David Barrett," he said, "and this is my wife, Marnie."

When Mrs. Oberle looked at Marnie, her mouth fell open, and she grasped the doorframe for support. "Oh my God! Martha told me she had a twin sister, but I can't believe how much you look like her."

Chapter 39

"Twin?" Marnie sputtered as she clung harder to David's arm. "I'm her twin?"

"Oh, you poor thing!" Mrs. Oberle said. "I didn't mean to shock you. Please, come in and sit down." She held the door wide for them to enter. "I forgot you had lost your memory."

David helped Marnie inside. The feeling of being in the middle of a twirling top intensified until she rested and drank the glass of water Mrs. Oberle had given to her. "I think I'm OK now. Please continue."

"Your husband told me you didn't have any memory of your past, but I didn't realize it was so severe. I truly didn't mean to shock you like that."

"That's all right, Mrs. Oberle. You didn't know. You see, I don't even know what caused me to lose my memory. The doctor said it was some kind of trauma, but we don't know, without me remembering the past, what it was. So I don't even know if I knew before the amnesia that I have a twin sister. Would you tell me about her, please?"

"She's a lovely person—I'll say that first off—a lovely person. A lady. And she's had some bad things happen in her life. She looks just like you, or you look just like her, whichever way you want to put it." Mrs. Oberle looked at Marnie and smiled. "I've known twins before like that. Once you get to know them, you can tell the difference, but at first it's a real shock.

"Martha started renting from me almost a year ago. You see, after my children were all grown and my husband passed away, I divided my house into two living spaces to have a little extra income. She rented the apartment." She nodded toward the wall. "Has a good job, she does, and had good references, too."

"Tell us about Ms. Kelley going missing," David said.

"I didn't realize she was missing at first. She travels with her job, so I didn't think much about it," replied Mrs. Oberle. She turned toward Marnie. "She's a sales rep for a company that sells things to big hotels: furniture, sheets, towels, and all sorts of things they use. She travels all over the country doing that."

Turning back to David, she continued, "She came down with the flu, that bad kind that's been going around. It knocked her for a loop, let me tell you. Put her flat in bed, not able to work a lick. She was pretty run-down before she took sick, so that's probably why it hit her so hard. She was thin, and she said she didn't sleep well. She worked hard, I'll grant you that. It's like she tried to work hard so she wouldn't have time to think about anything else. When I didn't see her up and around, I thought she had gone back to work and was just gone on one of her sales trips.

"Are you saying that this is when she disappeared? She wasn't gone on a sales trip?"

"Yes. That's what I'm trying to explain. She usually tells me when she's leaving, but I thought she'd just forgotten this time, so I wasn't worried at first.

"But then the first of the month came, and the rent was due. Now I trust her to pay the rent—she'd never been late, not once—and I thought she'd pay it once she got back. But she didn't come back. I started getting worried, and I got her rental application out of my file and looked up the number of the company she worked for and called them. I was thinking she might have fallen sick in some other city—maybe even been put in the hospital somewhere.

"They said she hadn't come back to work. Her boss said they were thinking she was still home, sick. That's when I called the police. They came out and looked all over the apartment."

"The police detective called us," David explained. "They found a slip of paper with my wife's name and phone number on it and thought maybe she knew what had happened. Of course, the police didn't know about them being sisters—twins at that.

"But with my wife's memory loss, she couldn't tell them a thing. We came to Phoenix hoping something here would help her remember. It's possible her memory loss and her sister's disappearance are tied together somehow."

"My goodness!" the older woman exclaimed. She drew back and stared at Marnie.

"I'd like to ask you something else," David said, drawing a picture from his jacket pocket. "Have you ever seen this man around here—around Ms. Kelley?"

Mrs. Oberle took the picture and studied it. "No, I can't say as I've ever seen him before, but that don't mean much. I've got a little sitting room in the back of the house where I spend most of my time. I don't see anyone who comes and goes next door, but I don't think she has much company. She's a loner—except for her job, of course." She handed the picture back. "I've never known her to date, or even to go out with a girlfriend. But, like I said, I don't know everything that goes on. It's not any of my business. I try not to be a nosy landlady."

"I wonder if we could look at her apartment," David asked. "Maybe we'll see something we recognize that would have no significance to the police."

"Well . . ." Mrs. Oberle paused to think about the request. "I guess as long as I stayed with you it'd be OK." Her concern showed in her eyes. "Not that I think you'd take anything, but you're strangers to me, after all, and I can't just let strangers rummage around in her things. You understand?"

"Certainly," David reassured her. "I understand. It would perfectly fine for you to be with us. In fact, I would prefer it."

"Let me go get the key."

She disappeared down a hallway. While she was gone, David questioned Marnie.

"Well? Does any of this seem familiar?"

"Yes, it does! Mrs. Oberle seems familiar to me, and this house does, too. But if I came here and met my sister, if I met Mrs. Oberle, then why doesn't she remember me?"

"I don't know. Maybe you saw her from a distance, and she didn't see you. Or maybe your sister has a picture of Mrs. Oberle in her apartment."

"She doesn't remember seeing Ray, either."

"No, she doesn't. But as she said, she doesn't see who comes and goes at your sister's."

The landlady returned, her house slippers slapping the tiled floor as she entered the room.

"Found it! Sometimes I don't put it back where I usually keep it. Then I have to hunt. I had it out for the police and didn't put it back in the drawer of my desk, like I ought to have. Come on. Let's go next door. Maybe something you see will tell us where she went. I tell you, I'm plum worried about her. I hope nothing bad has happened."

They went out the front door and along the covered porch until they reached the other blue door. As Mrs. Oberle was fitting the key into the lock, Marnie asked, "Her first name, is it Martha?"

The door swung open, and Mrs. Oberle stepped back to let them enter.

"Yes, that was her first name all right, but she went by her nickname—Martie."

Chapter 40

When she stepped inside the door to the apartment, she was bombarded with images and sounds, seen and heard only by her. It was as if dozens of movies were playing at once all around the room, along with radios blaring strange conversations with unfamiliar voices, none of which made any sense, and the room whirled around her. *No! No! Don't! Let go of me! There's someone who wants to hurt me! They're going to make me . . . make me . . . what? I've got to get away! I've got to get away from . . . .* Terror threatened to take over. It took all of Marnie's resistance to withstand its power.

It was an ordinary room, small and furnished with a tan couch and an overstuffed side chair. A colorful afghan was tossed across the back of the couch, and a book lay on an end table. It looked, to Marnie, like a comfortable place to sit and read—not a scary place at all. Off to the side, through an arched doorway, was a dining room, although it looked as if it was being used as an office. The table held stacks of papers and file folders. A cup kept a supply of pens and pencils close at hand.

Mrs. Oberle was speaking. "That lamp there," she said, pointing to a table lamp by the front door, "was on the floor." She turned toward the dining room. "There were papers all over the floor, and this chair"—she advanced into the room and put her hand on the back of one of the chairs sitting at the table—"it was turned over. When the police came, they took pictures of everything then they told me I could straighten it up."

Memories hovered around the edges, trying to gain entrance to Marnie's consciousness. She felt as if she had to get away from someone. Her eyes darted one way and another, looking for escape, until they lit on the framed photographs sitting on a table in the living room, and the dam finally broke.

Rushing to the pictures, she snatched one up and held it to her chest as sobs rose in her throat and a piercing cry burst forth. Overcome, she almost fell to her knees, but the man with her put his arm around her and led her to the sofa. It took Marnie a minute to remember David's name, the flood of memories was so strong.

He sat beside her and pulled her against his chest, making comforting sounds as he held her close, placing his cheek on the top of her head.

But she could not be comforted, and the billowing sobs continued until she didn't have the strength to utter another sound.

"Should I call the doctor?" the landlady asked.

"No. I think not," David said. "I think it's her memory coming back. It's upset her, but it had to happen at some point. The doctor back home who saw her said something traumatic had caused her amnesia, and it might be traumatic to regain her past. Giving her a sedative might knock her out and prevent her from remembering. I can get her one later if she needs it. I'd say something happened to her in this room. Who is the little boy in the picture she's holding?"

The sobbing had eased somewhat, and before Mrs. Oberle answered, she struggled to speak. "D . . . Da . . . David. I'm not . . . not who you think I am."

"Shh . . . sweetheart, it's OK. I told you, we'll work through whatever it is, whatever you did."

"N . . . no! No! David . . . I'm not your wife," she stuttered amid the sobs.

She pulled herself away from him, and loosening her grasp on the picture, she gazed at the little blond boy in the photograph.

"I . . . I lost him. I lost my baby . . . and now I've lost Jonathan, too."

"What?" David couldn't follow the train of thought.

Still looking at the picture, she answered. "This was my son, Thomas. Tommy. And he's dead!" Tears that had lessened started to roll down her face once again. "And Jonathan isn't my son, so I'll lose him, too."

"Then you aren't . . . aren't Marnie?" David asked.

She shook her head, trying to still her shuddering voice.

"No. I'm Martie." She buried her face in his chest, unable to speak any more.

David looked to Mrs. Oberle and raised his eyebrows.

"My goodness, what a turn! I thought she looked just like Martie when I answered the door. And sure enough, she was." She frowned at David. "Do you mean you didn't know it wasn't your wife? That seems strange to me. Wouldn't you recognize your own wife, or rather, know when it wasn't her?"

"I knew . . . I knew she was different somehow, but she looks just like Marnie except that she was pale and thin. Her actions and words—her personality—were different, but she had lost all her memories, and although I thought it was odd she acted dissimilar to how she had been, after a while I accepted it.

"You see, my wife, Marnie, had run away with another man—the man in the picture I showed you. I was very angry and upset because, not only had she left me and our son, but also because she and the man, Ray, had stolen something very valuable from me, and I had to find it."

"Well, how in the world did Martie end up with you thinking she's your wife?"

"When she showed up, everyone assumed she Marnie—the doctor, who has known her since she was a child, and everyone in the household. We told her that's who she was, and she just accepted it. You don't realize how identical they are!"

"But how did she come to be there where you live?"

"That's what I'd like to know," David said, "and I'd like to find out where Marnie and Ray are."

Martie lifted her head from David's chest.

"They were here," she said. The tears were spent, and she could speak once again. The memories weren't flooding back but were returning one by one. "They wanted me to pretend to be her, to throw you off trying to find them by giving false information."

"Had you been in touch with Marnie all along?"

"No. She got in touch with me not long before they showed up here. She said she wanted to meet me and was coming to visit."

"You weren't in contact with your identical twin sister?" Mrs. Oberle asked.

"No. In fact, I only learned of her existence a few months ago and had no idea how to get in touch with her. I was surprised when she called me. Surprised and thrilled. I was excited over the prospect of meeting her."

"So she and Ray showed up here?" David asked.

"Yes, and they said they wanted me to do something for them. They wanted me to pretend I was Marnie, but I said I wouldn't do it. They tried very hard to persuade me, but I kept refusing. Finally, they lost patience with me, and the man, Ray, grabbed me, and they both held me down while he gave an injection of some sort. I passed out. The next thing I remember I was standing at the top of a hill—the hill at the back of the park. I wandered down to the park, and you know the story from there."

Chapter 41

An hour later they were back at the hotel. Martie felt both uncomfortable and relieved to be with David. She had argued that since she was not his wife she ought to stay at her own home even though the thought of being alone frightened her. Too much had happened there, and it made her nervous and upset. Still, she didn't feel right staying with a married man, much less one married to her sister. But David insisted she remain with him. Her emotional state was too fragile, he argued, for her to be alone, and he didn't want her to be at her apartment in case Marnie and Ray returned for any reason.

"In reality," he added, "I want to keep you near me because it feels right, like it's where you belong, close to me. I have fought, these last weeks, not to fall in love with the woman I believed was Marnie, but evidently I haven't fought hard enough. You are in my heart, and not because of, but in spite of thinking you were my wife."

It was comforting to have David close by, to listen when she wanted to talk and to hold her when she cried. He would help her get through anything that came along, but she felt guilty using her sister's husband in that way. She needed him, though, really needed him to keep her from breaking down. She needed him to assure her that everything was going to be all right. Being alone was unthinkable.

David immediately called Detective Mendez and told him they had located Ms. Kelley—she had been visiting relatives in Colorado and everything was OK. "That is the simplest way to handle it," David explained to Martie. "If it turns out to be something the Phoenix police would get involved with, I'll try to explain more at that time."

"Let's start at the beginning. You can tell me anything you want to. Take your time, and try to not get upset. If it gets too hard, stop for a while."

Martie was lying on the king-sized bed, a wet washcloth covering her swollen eyes. The puffy duvet felt cool to her skin, and the air conditioner hummed softly in the background. She removed the cloth and sat up.

"OK"—she folded the cloth—"but where to start?"

"Any place you want to," David answered.

She wandered to the window and looked down upon the city.

"I guess I should start when I was little girl." She sat in a nearby chair. "Although some of this I just learned recently.

"My parents, I guess I should say *our* parents, divorced when we were little. Evidently it was a very acrimonious parting. Neither one of them wanted to see the other one ever again. But, if Marnie and I were kept together, there would be constant visitations and switching us back and forth, and they would have to deal with each other for years. So they split us up. I went with our father, and Marnie went with our mother.

"By the way, you might be interested to know that Marnie is not your wife's real name."

"Not her real name?" David said, amazed. He walked over and sat in the chair facing Martie.

"No. My name is really Martha, and Marnie's real name is Marnetta. We were named for a couple of aunts we had never met. Anyway, we ended up being called Martie and Marnie from babyhood on.

"We were young when we were separated, but as I grew up, I vaguely remembered having a sister. My father refused to talk about her, though, and brushed the subject aside anytime I asked about her or my mother. Eventually, I came to the conclusion they had both died and it was too painful for my father to talk about. I was wrong, of course."

"When did you find out Marnie was still alive?"

"Some time after my father's death, when I received a letter from my father's lawyer. Let me skip over that part for a while."

"OK."

"I had a perfectly normal childhood and adolescence. I grew up and fell in love and got married." She stopped talking and put her hand to her mouth, holding in the sob that threatened.

"You don't have to talk about it if you don't want to," David said and started to stretch out his hand to her, but he pulled back.

"No, it's OK," she said. She got up and walked to the bathroom to get another tissue. "I have to tell it."

When she returned, she continued the story. "Greg was my college sweetheart, but I didn't really know him as well as I ought to have before getting married. We should never have married. He wasn't ready to settle down and be a husband and father. The best thing about the marriage was our son, Thomas." She paused again as tears silently rolled down her cheeks.

David reached over and took her hand in his.

"I have to know. Are you still married?"

A great shuddering sob shook her, and it took a moment before she could answer.

"No. He's dead. He and my baby, my Tommy, are dead. And when they died, I wanted to die along with them."

"What happened? Can you tell me? Or is it too painful?"

"It'll be painful, but it feels good to be able to talk about it. All this time, I've had nobody to talk to. I didn't want to tell such personal things to casual friends."

"You don't have to tell me, either, if you don't want to."

"David, I want to tell you. You're the first person I've wanted to talk to since I came to after the wreck and realized I was still alive but my baby wasn't."

Chapter 42

"By the time Greg and I graduated from college, we had only been dating about six months or so, but we were in love and didn't want to be separated when we went out into the 'real world,'" Martie said, using her fingers to make air quotes. "So we went to Las Vegas and got married. I must admit I felt kind of alone in the world, and it was very comforting to have someone by my side as I went out there to find a job and an apartment."

"Where was your father? Wasn't he around?" David asked.

"Dad was there, sort of, and he cautioned me about jumping into marriage too soon. From things he said, I got the notion he and my mother had done so, although I still was under the impression she and my sister were dead. But the sad thing was, by that time my father was beginning to show signs of Alzheimer's disease, which would later overcome him entirely. When I tried to talk with him, he couldn't stay on the subject, couldn't remember what we had talked about the day before. It took everything he had to get through each day. I offered to move in with him, to help him, but that suggestion angered him. So when Greg and I married, we got an apartment close by so I could check on him often.

"It wasn't long, though, before he had to enter a nursing home, and even though I visited often, he ended up not recognizing me at all."

"That must have been very sad for you," David commented.

"Yes, it was. At first I was happy I had Greg to depend on. We both had good jobs. I was a sales rep for a paper goods company, and Greg sold computer systems to big corporations.

We were doing well financially, and when I got pregnant, we bought a house. 'A big house for a big family' is what we said. We were so happy to have a baby on the way." She smiled at the thought, but soon her face was sad once again.

"But all the good times changed when it became obvious something was wrong in our lives, something to do with finances. When Tommy was almost a year old, I hired someone to come in and care for him, and I went back to work. Greg and I both had well-paying jobs and ought to have been able to easily support our lifestyle. But, all of a sudden, bills weren't getting paid, and collection agencies started calling."

"That must have been rough," David sympathized.

"Yes, it was. When I questioned Greg, he would say it was just a mistake, a foul-up in accounting, but when the foreclosure notice came on the house, I knew it wasn't a mistake. By this time we were fighting all the time. I had already threatened to leave him, to take Tommy with me, and he said I'd never keep him from his son. But the worst was when the men came to the door looking for him."

"Men?" David straightened abruptly. "Who were they? What did they want?"

"They wanted Greg. They wanted the money he had borrowed from their boss. And they wanted it right then.

"It seems Greg had developed a gambling habit. Sometimes, when I thought he was on a sales trip, he was in Las Vegas gambling and losing. When he ran through all our savings, he borrowed money, and the men were there to collect on past due payments."

"My God," David exclaimed, sitting back in his chair. "It sounds like something out of a movie."

"Well, I'll never again enjoy that kind of movie. They were insistent, and I was frightened. I confronted Greg over it, and he admitted what was going on. We were about to lose everything we had. There was no one to go to, nowhere to turn."

Martie wished David would gather her in his arms, kiss her, and tell her not to worry, that he would take care of everything. But the reality of the situation was that he was not her husband—he was her brother-in-law. She had no right to be in his arms, no right to kiss him.

"What happened next?" he asked grimly.

"I consulted an attorney about a divorce. That wouldn't have helped the existing debts, but if we were divorced, any new debts Greg accumulated wouldn't be my problem. We were filing for bankruptcy. Greg insisted bankruptcy wouldn't solve a thing with the men, 'goons' he called them, who were out to collect the debt he owed their boss.

"We were fighting about custody of Tommy—I wanted custody with visitation for Greg—when he showed up at the house one day, picked up Tommy, and walked out with him."

"My God! What did you do?"

"I rushed out after them. I couldn't physically stop him, so I got into the car with them. I might not be able to stop him from taking Tommy, but, I reasoned, if I was with them, at least I'd know where Tommy was—be with him."

"What was Greg's plan? What did he think he could gain by snatching Tommy?"

"I don't think he had a plan. He had been drinking and decided to take his son. That was it, plain and simple. He wanted his son, so he took him.

"We were arguing. I was trying to convince Greg to take us back to the house, and he was telling me he wouldn't do it. He was driving faster and faster, and the more I begged him to slow down, the faster he went. He was weaving in and out of traffic, passing cars with little room to get back in line.

"Tommy was in the back seat." Her voice broke as she recalled that day. "He wasn't even in a car seat. I kept telling him to put the seatbelt on and pull it tight, and he was scared and crying. 'Make Daddy slow down,' he begged me. 'He's scaring me.'"

She took a deep, shaky breath. "That was the last thing my baby ever said."

David reached over and took her hand, holding it in both of his.

"When I looked back at the road, he had pulled out to pass a car, and there, coming toward us, was a big rig with its brakes screeching, headed right toward us. Greg tried to pull back into the right lane, but he hit the car that was there. The last thing I remember was heading into that collision—lots of pain—rolling over and over—then blackness."

Chapter 43

David got to his feet, and taking both of Martie's hands, he drew her up out of her chair and into his arms. Her tears dampened his shirt as she wept silently. After a couple of minutes, Martie put distance between them. "Let me finish telling you," she said. She squeezed his hands then released them and sat back down in her seat. David went back to his chair.

"When I woke up in the hospital, I found out I had been unconscious for two months. My husband and child were dead and buried. I had no one and nothing. The bank had foreclosed on the house. With me not able to cooperate, the bankruptcy couldn't proceed. Finally, everything was sold— all the furniture and paintings and everything else Greg and I had bought during our marriage.

"I was able to collect my clothes and personal items. All of Tommy's furniture and toys were sold at auction along with the rest of the furnishings. I was able to keep some of his books and a couple of toys. Those few things and the pictures of him are all that I have." She thought about the fact she no longer had a right to Jonathan, either, and her eyes filled with tears once again.

"During that last day, when everything was being auctioned, the two men, the 'goons', showed up again."

"What did they want? With Greg dead you'd think they'd have given up."

"Not a chance. They were convinced Greg must have had some life insurance that would come to me. They made it plain I still owed Greg's debt. That's when I really got scared."

"Did you tell the police about it?"

"Yes, I did, but they didn't sound like they could do anything about it."

David swore under his breath. "What did you do?"

"For all intents and purposes, I disappeared. I took back my maiden name, Kelley, and started using my real first name, Martha, instead of Martie, for any official business. The bankruptcy went through under my married name, so when that was over, I was free of debt. I had nothing, but I owed nothing."

"That's something, I guess. Lots of people have to start over from the beginning," David said.

"Yes, that's what I thought, too. I got a new job. My old company held mine as long as they could but finally hired someone else to take my place. I scraped up enough money for a month's rent and found the apartment at Mrs. Oberle's house. I found a new job quick enough—I was good at what I did and had excellent references. I was a rep for a big firm that sold hotel supplies all over the country. You name it, I sold it. It kept me on the road, or on an airplane, but I didn't mind.

"I was doing well enough. I kept busy with my work so I wouldn't have to think about the past. I had no friends and didn't want any. They might ask me about my life, and I couldn't talk about it. You're the first person I've been able to tell all this to."

"So how do Marnie and Ray come into the story?" David asked.

Martie sighed. "I'll get to them in a minute.

"I hadn't been living at Mrs. Oberle's very long when my father died. That was something else I added to my list of things to put out of my mind. If I didn't, I would be overwhelmed with grief. I went through his funeral closed off from the world.

"Luckily, he had made all the plans years before when he found out the diagnosis of Alzheimer's, so I didn't have to deal with that. A few weeks later I received a letter from his attorney. In it was a letter my father had written to me before his memory got too bad. It told me about my mother and Marnie."

David leaned forward, fascinated with the story.

"He told me my mother's name was Pamela, something I hadn't known before then, and he told me about my identical twin sister. He said although the marriage was a disaster, I was a blessing to him and that he loved me dearly." She touched a tissue to her eyes before continuing.

"There was a big age difference between him and Pamela, he said, and he ought to have thought it over more before marrying her. They were thrilled to have twin daughters, and each named one after an aunt of theirs. I was named Martha after an aunt of his, and my sister was named Marnetta for one of my mother's aunts, but we immediately became Martie and Marnie.

"We weren't very old when they divorced, maybe three or so. When they split up, neither of them wanted to see the other one again, so they split us up, too. That was a terrible plan," she said angrily, "separating us that way. Terrible not to know your identical twin all your life."

"Yes, yes it was," David murmured.

"David, what was Marnie's maiden name? Pamela's name? Was it Kelley?"

"No, Kelley would have rung a bell with me when I heard your name if that had been it." He closed his eyes and thought a minute. "Caldwell. Pamela and Marnie Caldwell."

"My father's letter said Pamela left him for another man, and a few months later he gave permission for her new husband to adopt Marnie. I guess he did.

"I don't know what happened then, because Doctor Means said Marnie was about six when he first started seeing her, and Alice said she was about that age when they moved in across the hall." Martie smiled for the first time that day. "You don't know how hard it is not to say I and me instead of she and her, since I was sort of Marnie when they told me all that."

David chuckled.

"Anyway, Dad's letter said he wanted me to know I had a mother and an identical twin sister somewhere in the country, although he had no idea where they had gone. I guess Caldwell died, or they got a divorce, too."

"I guess so. I never heard anything about a husband or ex-husband in connection with Pamela," David said.

"So now we are coming to the part about Marnie and Ray," Martie said.

"Yes, I want to know how they found you and what they wanted from you."

"About six months ago, I had been working on a big sale to a hotel in Los Angeles, and I was hurrying across the lobby. I needed to catch a plane, and I was in a rush when a man called to me. He said, 'Hey there. What are you doing in Los Angeles? You didn't mention it the other night.'

"I told him he must have the wrong person, that I didn't know him. He stared at me like I was crazy, so I pulled out a business card and gave it to him and told him I had to catch a plane and left. After I got settled on the plane, I was disappointed I hadn't taken the time to question him. I thought then that he might have known my sister. I kicked myself for passing up the opportunity."

"Was it . . .?"

She nodded. "Yes, it was Ray."

Chapter 44

"And he went back home and told Marnie he saw someone who looked just like her," David surmised.

"Yes, and she might have known already she had a twin sister," Martie said.

"If she didn't, the fact that someone out there looked enough like her to be her twin fit into their plans, whatever they were. What happened next?" David asked. "When did they get in touch with you? And what did they want you to do?"

"A few weeks later, Marnie called me. We talked a while. I was so happy to have been contacted by my twin. I had been thinking about my father's letter and wondering how in the world I would go about finding her, and here she was calling me. She said her friend saw me and told her about it. I'm pretty sure I'm the one who mentioned knowing I had an identical twin sister somewhere, so I don't know for sure if she knew about having a twin before that conversation or not. We talked for a few minutes, and she said she would call me back so we could talk some more. She called back a week or two later. She said she had a plan. She wondered if I'd like to switch places, like the girls in the movie did, to see if people could tell the difference. She said it would be fun."

"Huh," David said.

"I didn't think it was a very 'fun' sounding thing to do, but I didn't tell her just like that. I said I was busy working but that I hoped we could meet some day just to visit and compare notes about our lives.

"She said she would tell me all about her life, that it would make it easier for me to pretend to be her. That's when

I told her I didn't think I wanted to do that. She said for me to think about it, and she kept insisting it would be a fun thing to do. I took down her name and phone number so I could call her, 'if you change your mind,' she said."

"So they were planning something involving switching places," David mused. "That must have been the paper the Phoenix police said they found when they called me. But by that time, Marnie's cell phone had been turned off, probably so we couldn't track her with it. The police traced who the phone number belonged to and that led to me, since I paid the bill for the phone. That's how they found me."

Martie continued her story. "By then I had come down with the flu and was very sick. I was in bed for days, and I was just getting back on my feet when Marnie and Ray showed up. At first I was absolutely thrilled to meet my sister. I would never have believed the two of us could look so much alike, especially not having been raised together."

"You certainly are. I'm embarrassed that I didn't recognize you weren't my wife."

Martie looked down at her lap, picking some imaginary lint, when she spoke. "Well, I gather you and Marnie hadn't shared a bedroom in some months. Maybe the memories faded somewhat."

"That's true, but still . . ." David looked discomfited with the idea he had thought this woman was his wife.

"If you had no idea there was a twin in the picture, how could you have guessed it wasn't Marnie who came to your door?" Martie reasoned.

"So when they showed up at *your* door, what did they say their plan was?" David asked, changing the focus off his wrong assumption.

"At first we just visited. I told her I had been married but that my husband had been killed in a car wreck. I didn't—couldn't—go into details. She told me she was married and had a son. She didn't go into detail either. She said it was important she be absent from her family for a few days, but it was equally important that people believe she was still there. It was a business matter, she said."

"They offered me ten thousand dollars to pretend to be her. When I said no, they raised it to twenty thousand. She told me you didn't share a bedroom, so I didn't have to worry about that, and she said a nanny cared for her son, so I wouldn't have anything to do but lie around. I could use her car and her credit cards to get anything I wanted, plus the money they'd pay me. I still said no.

"And then Ray said, 'We're going to have to insist,' and he grabbed me. I struggled. That's when the chair got turned over and the papers scattered. He held me, and Marnie pulled a hypodermic needle out of her purse and gave me a shot of something. Everything was fading to black when Ray carried me to their car. I think I remember the lamp hitting the floor as he carried me out the door."

"My God, they were not only serious, they had planned it so thoroughly they came prepared with something to put you out," David marveled. "Do you remember anything after that?"

"Just vague memories, ones that may not be accurate. I remember sort of waking up and being in a small airplane. Ray and Marnie were discussing what they were going to do, and Ray was saying, 'We'll just put her out there. She can see town from there, and she'll find her way down. It isn't hard, for heaven's sake. Stop worrying about her.' When they saw I was awake, Marnie gave me another shot.

"The next thing I remember was being in some sort of vehicle, driving on a bumpy road. I woke up in a grove of trees in the park, and you know the story from there."

Chapter 45

They talked for hours. Marnie went over every step of her abduction several times, hoping to remember some detail, something she overheard, that might give David a clue about Marnie and Ray's next step.

When she had repeated her story several times, she talked about her earlier life.

"I had a good childhood. Daddy was a good father, and although I wished I had a mother like most of my friends, I didn't really suffer because I didn't have one. Several of my schoolmates were divorced, so it didn't seem unusual to have only one parent. My best friend's parents were divorced, and she lived with her mother. She envied me because I had a father."

They talked about her marriage to Greg and how different he turned out to be than the man she thought she had married.

"When I found out my parents were divorced, I spent a lot of time thinking about marriage, and I wondered if that was what had happened to my parents. Maybe they married thinking the other one was someone completely different than who they turned out to be."

"After all I've been through, I can say I should never have married Marnie, although I am thankful for Jonathan. He's the best thing that ever happened to me.

"And Marnie wasn't all bad. She was kind and sympathetic when my father and uncle died and I was under so much stress trying to run the business." He looked at Martie and smiled. "The way she was then reminds me of you, except she was only that way for a while, and you're that way all the time. She was Marnie with a little touch of Martie in her personality. You are Martie with a little touch of Marnie from time to time."

Martie shuddered. "I hope I'm not too much like her. From what I've heard, I'd rather be me, all Martie."

"I'm glad you're Martie, too," Davie said, passion exuding from his voice.

They looked away from each other, both realizing the delicate situation they were in.

"I'm getting hungry," David said, standing and stretching. "Let's go to the coffee shop and get something to eat."

Readily agreeing, Martie fixed her hair and makeup, and they went downstairs. After ordering, they sat silently, thinking about all that had occurred in the last twenty-four hours. So many questions were still unanswered, and their lives were even more scrambled than when they thought she was Marnie.

Finally, Martie asked, "So, where do we go from here?"

David started to reach for her hands and then withdrew his to his lap.

"I think you need to come back home with me."

"But I have no place there. I'm not your wife." Her voice almost caught at the thought. "And I need to get back to my own life. I need to see if I still have a job."

"I'll tell you two reasons you need to come back with me. One is those two goons could still be looking for you. I don't like the idea of them finding you. I don't like it at all."

"They haven't found me yet, and it's been a while."

"That doesn't mean they aren't still looking."

Martie thought about that as she ate. "What's the second reason?"

"Jonathan. Remember when I thought you were Marnie and I told you I wouldn't let you hurt him again? Well, I still won't. You can't just drop out of his life . . . like his mother did."

Martie put down her sandwich and wiped her mouth. The thought of leaving Jonathan was tearing at her heart.

"The thought of losing Jonathan is almost as bad as the hurt I felt when Tommy was killed."

"You won't lose him, I promise."

"But he is Marnie's child, not mine, and she will have something to say about how close I can be to him."

"When I find Marnie, she is in so much hot water she will have no option but to do as I say about Jonathan or anything else."

"Can you bear to put her in jail? Can you really send the mother of your child to jail?"

David pushed his plate away and crossed his arms on the table. "I don't know. I thought I could . . . before you. I was filled with so much anger because of how she had treated her son and me. Her running away with Ray and them out to get rich on the downfall of Barrett's Enterprises was just too much to ever forgive. Now, I feel . . . I don't know . . . not forgiving, exactly, but not as filled with thoughts of revenge."

"I think I've changed, too. All these months filled with sadness and pain, I couldn't let go of the anger I felt for Greg. I blamed myself for so much . . . for not keeping Tommy safe and for marrying Greg in the first place . . . for not seeing what was happening long before I did.

"Now I feel as if it has all been released—all the crying and remorse I felt when I thought I was Marnie and all the emotion that ran through me when my memory came back. All those tears washed away the past. I feel stronger now. I feel new. I think the past is behind me at last."

"Anything else for you folks?" the waitress asked as she placed their ticket on the table.

"No, thanks," David replied. He looked around the room. "It looks like they are trying to close up. I guess it's time to leave." He placed some bills on the table, and they went back out into the lobby of the hotel.

"Are you going to want me to get another room?" he asked.

"Do you *want* to get another room?"

"No. I want to stay with you."

Martie sighed. "I want you with me, but I keep thinking about the fact you are my sister's husband."

"I promise I won't touch you. I'll even sleep on the floor if you want me to." David's look was beseeching.

Martie laughed. "That won't be necessary. That king-sized bed is big enough for two people." Her expression was serious as they stepped from the elevator. "To be honest, I'm still kind of shaky from all this. I'd feel better knowing you are there."

It'll be the last night I'll ever be this close to him, she thought. *Even not touching, it's better than being alone and him in another room.*

Chapter 46

Martie woke up the next morning when David unwrapped his arms from around her and eased out of bed. She didn't know when they had tangled themselves together. When she fell asleep, David was on the far right of the bed and she was on the far left. She only knew she felt bereft when he withdrew his warm embrace and left the bed.

"Good morning," he said when he returned from the bathroom, fully dressed, and noticed she was awake. "Sleep well?"

"I slept perfectly, thank you."

"I'm going to go down and get a cup of coffee. Why don't you join me there when you're ready?" he asked.

"OK," Martie answered, thinking about the coffee maker in their room.

Is he being thoughtful, trying to lessen any stress on me by leaving me alone to dress, or is he trying to distance himself from me?

Nothing to do but play it out, she thought. *So what if he does want to distance himself. He is married to someone else, after all.*

A half an hour later she spotted him in a corner booth, drinking coffee and reading the morning paper.

"Hi," he said with a smile, as she slid into the seat opposite him. "Would you like some breakfast?"

"Just orange juice and wheat toast, please," she said to the waitress who approached with a pot of coffee.

"I've been thinking about what to do next," David said.

"Tell me."

"I want to go see Mrs. Oberle again and give her a check for the rent you owe plus another month. That will give us some time to organize our thoughts. Since we now know Ray and Marnie were here in Phoenix, maybe that will give the private detective more clues to find them. For example, they had to have rented a car to get to your house, and they probably stayed at some hotel or motel here. Maybe someone at one of those places remembers something they said or did that would lead us to them."

"That's all great except that I'm the one who needs to pay the rent. It's my apartment after all."

"We can straighten that out later, but for now let me pay." Martie opened her mouth to object, but he quickly added, "You haven't been working, and your bank account might be kind of low."

Martie quickly shut her mouth as the truth of that statement hit home.

"Secondly, it was through the hands of my wife you suffered amnesia and kidnapping. If not for that, you would have been home all this time, working and living a normal life. Consider this as payment for damages caused by Marnie's actions."

The waitress brought Martie's breakfast and set it before her. She buttered the toast while thinking about what David had said.

"OK," she said at last. "At least for now."

"We can gather up anything you want from your place to take back with you. You must have a suitcase since you travel with your work. You can fill it with anything you'd like.

"I'd like to keep it as close to normal as possible with Jonathan, and he's expecting you to come back to him. We can go on as we have been, if that's all right with you." It sounded more like a question than a statement.

"If you mean as we were before we went to the cabin, then OK," Martie replied. As much as David tempted her, she wouldn't fall back into the bed of a man she knew was married to someone else.

After a few tense moments, David finally spoke. "Yes, the way it was before we went up to the cabin—friendly, but with separate bedrooms. There's an early afternoon flight back. I've booked us on it. I can always cancel if this doesn't meet with your approval."

"That's fine with me," she said as she finished the last of her juice. "I'm ready."

They spent some time with Mrs. Oberle, but they didn't tell her about Marnie and Ray kidnapping Martie.

"Martie is coming back home with me," David told the older woman. "That way she'll be there when my wife shows up. Martie has grown close to my son, caring for him in my wife's absence, and he'd miss her if she stays here."

"But I plan on coming back here," Martie assured Mrs. Oberle, hoping David understood, too. "Since I've been wearing my sister's clothes up until now, I'm going to take some of my own."

"But tell me again, how did you get to thinking you were your sister?" Mrs. Oberle couldn't figure out the complicated story of identical twins.

"She lost her memory," David explained. "Possibly from the earlier trauma of the injuries in the wreck that killed her husband and son and then the severe case of the flu." He left out the part where Ray and Marnie kidnapped her. "When she showed up, she looked so much like Marnie everyone thought that's who she was. She was very sick. She accepted what we all told her."

He stood up and offered his hand to Mrs. Oberle. "Thank you so much for keeping Martie's apartment," he said, trying to steer the conversation away from the kidnapping. "We'll be back in touch with you before the rent is due again."

"I don't mind telling you I'm glad to get this check," she said, waving the piece of paper. "I didn't know what to do about the apartment. I was about ready to pack up all your things," she said, looking at Martie. "Of course I'd a kept them for you, but I need the money I get from renting out the place. I was thinking I needed to get someone else in there. I'm glad you're back. You've been the perfect tenant."

Once back in her apartment, Martie went directly to the bedroom and took the suitcase standing in the corner and placed it on the bed.

"I'll be glad to have my own clothes," she said as she filled it with items from the closet and drawers. "That's one thing I don't share with my sister, our taste in clothing."

"You always looked nice wearing her clothes," David commented as he watched her. "Although I must admit, I never saw Marnie wearing any of the things you chose to wear."

"Maybe she bought them and then decided she didn't like them," Martie said as she added a pile of underthings to the suitcase. "If I think about it when I see her again, I'll ask her."

"I'm not going to be thinking about her taste in clothes when I find her," David said grimly.

Martie knelt on the carpeted floor and opened the bottom drawer of the bureau. She withdrew a book and held it up for David to see. "Does this look familiar?" she asked.

"It's just like Jonathan's," he exclaimed.

"Yes, it is. When I read that book to Jonathan, when we discussed the dinosaurs, it always seemed familiar. That reinforced the idea I really was Marnie and Jonathan was my son. I thought I had read it to him before."

She turned and put it back in the drawer, tears threatening for the first time that day. "It was Tommy I had read it to, so many times we both had it about memorized." She withdrew a stuffed dinosaur from the drawer. "Tommy slept with this every night. I'm going to give it to Jonathan."

"You're sure?" David's eyes searched hers. "It means so much to you. Are you sure you want to give it up?"

"Yes. I'm sure. Jonathan means a lot to me, too. He'll like it, and it should be enjoyed by the cousin of the little boy who first loved it."

Chapter 47

They landed in Denver in the late afternoon. After retrieving their luggage and car, David suggested they eat supper before heading home. It was late before they reached their final destination, and the house was dark.

David helped Martie get her bags to her room and turned to leave.

"You know, it would be very embarrassing if Marnie came home and found me sleeping in her room," Martie said.

"If Marnie comes home she'll have a lot more to be concerned about than someone sleeping in her room," David answered. "Besides, she'd think her plan worked and you were pretending to be her, like she wanted in the first place."

"That's true."

She waited for David to leave, though she didn't want him to. She yearned for his arms around her and his kisses, but that was impossible now. She didn't know if things were better now that her memory was back or if they were worse. All she could do was see what happened next.

"Well, good night," David said.

"Good night," she answered. There was nothing more to say.

Martie slept late the next morning. By the time she rose, showered, and dressed, she missed having breakfast with Jonathan as she had planned. When she went to the playroom, David was holding Jonathan and telling him how glad he was to be home so they could play together.

When he saw Martie walk in, he turned to Mrs. Tucker. "Mrs. Tucker, could we have some time alone with Jonathan, please?"

"Certainly, Mr. Barrett. I'll be in my room." She picked up a piece of needlework and exited the playroom.

"I've brought you something," Martie said. She sat down in a chair and sat the stuffed dinosaur in her lap.

"For me?" Jonathan asked, eyes wide.

"For you," she agreed.

He climbed into her lap and took the stuffed animal, looking it over carefully.

"It's not new. It used to belong to another little boy who loved dinosaurs," she said.

"Doesn't he want it anymore?"

Martie took a deep breath before answering. She didn't want to cry in front of Jonathan.

"He . . . he died."

Jonathan studied her face, then looked back at the dinosaur.

"What was his name?"

"Tommy."

He studied the markings on the fabric toy, then said, "I'll take good care of it."

"I know you will," Martie said quietly and hugged him.

"Sport, we have something to tell you," David said. Jonathan looked at him quizzically.

"I know it's going to be hard to understand, but do you know how you thought this was your mother?" David motioned toward Martie.

Jonathan stared at his father. "No. She isn't my mother," he said as if correcting a preposterous statement.

David was nonplussed. "You didn't think she was your mother?"

"No. She looks kind of like my mother, but she's different. People kept saying she was my mother, but I knew she wasn't."

David looked at Martie, surprise written all over his face.

"How is she different?" he asked his son.

Jonathan didn't have to think about it long. "Well, she looks different. Her face is all smiley, and my mother's face isn't smiley. My mother smiles fake smiles sometimes, but she's not *smiley*." He emphasized the word to be sure they understood what he was saying.

"And this mommy is cuddly. My mother isn't cuddly. *And . . .*," he said importantly, "she *smells* different."

"Smells different?" David asked, befuddled over this turn of events.

"Yep. Different." Jonathan answered, looking back at the dinosaur and hugging it tight. "Was Tommy your little boy?" he asked Martie.

"Yes."

"I'm sorry he got dead."

She hugged him tight. "I am too, Jonathan. I am too."

After they had given Jonathan the set of dinosaur blocks they bought in the airport gift shop, they went downstairs for breakfast.

"You'd think I would have noticed you smell different," David said as they passed through the dining room.

"Shh. Someone might hear you," Martie said as she elbowed him.

When they entered the kitchen, they found Ruth, Mrs. Grady, and Alice. Ruth looked like she was on her way out, with her purse over her arm and car keys in her hand.

"Good morning, everybody," David greeted them.

"So you're home," Ruth said. "Has your wayward wife regained her memory?"

"In a way," David answered cryptically.

"In a way?" Ruth raised an eyebrow. "What does that mean?"

"It means this woman has regained her memory, but she's not my wife."

"You got a divorce while you were gone?" Ruth asked doubtfully.

"I mean, this isn't Marnie," David answered.

"Of course, she's Marnie. You're speaking nonsense."

"This is Marnie's identical twin sister, Martha Kelley—Martie," he said.

"Oh my," murmured Alice.

"My stars above," Mrs. Grady exclaimed.

"Rubbish!" Ruth said. "Another one of her tricks, and you fell for it, sounds like."

"No, I assure you, it's the truth," David said.

"So which one has been living here the last month?" Mrs. Grady asked.

"This one—Martie," he replied.

"Which one are you married to?" his mother asked.

"I'm married to Marnie."

"So what is this one doing here? Helping with the theft?"

"She's here because Marnie and Ray kidnapped her, drugged her, and put her out on City Park Hill to find her way down to town."

Ruth turned to Martie and said with a sneer, "So now you remember all this? You remember you aren't Marnie?"

"I didn't remember anything when I came here. Everyone told me I was Marnie Barrett, and I believed them."

"And suddenly you know who you are? A likely story!"

"I didn't remember until I entered my apartment in Phoenix and everything started rushing back. I had some pretty bad things happen to me, and I guess my mind just shut down and refused to remember anything at all."

"Well, I don't believe this cock-and-bull story, not a bit of it. Somehow you've convinced my son there are twins involved in this scam. Probably something went wrong between you and that man, Ray, and you've come back home with your tail between your legs hoping he'll take you back." She turned back to David. "I hope you are smarter than to believe this woman. She's taking you for a fool." She turned and started out of the kitchen.

"I've got to go. I'm meeting Celeste." She paused in the doorway. "Why you didn't marry Celeste as planned and let this . . . tramp . . . raise her bastard herself I'll never know."

Chapter 48

David shook his head. "I've talked enough. She'll never change her attitude." He looked at Martie. "I started to say 'toward you,' but I guess I mean toward both you and Marnie."

"I can't get over it," said Alice. "I've known Marnie since she was a little tyke, and I never guessed you weren't her."

"I guess you didn't know she had an identical twin, then, did you?"

"No, I didn't. Neither she nor Pamela ever mentioned such a thing."

"When my parents divorced, each took one of us. My father in Phoenix raised me. I didn't find out about having a twin until after my father died. He left a letter telling me about her."

Mrs. Grady started polishing the granite countertop. "You must have been a little thing if you don't remember that."

"Yes, I think we were about three when they separated."

David spoke up. "I brought Martie back here because she has established a relationship with Jonathan, and I didn't want him to think she had deserted him."

"That should've made me realize something was real different about you. Miss Marnie would never have spent so much time with Jonathan. She would never have spent so much time at home. Period," said Alice.

Just then the telephone rang. Mrs. Grady answered it and handed the receiver to David. After a brief conversation, he hung up.

"That was the sheriff," he said to Martie. "He was checking to see if I was here and if he could come by and talk to me. He said he has something important to tell me. He'll be right over."

"I'll wait here in the kitchen," Martie told him.

"No. I want you with me. After all, Marnie is your sister. You deserve to be informed of whatever he has found."

"Are you sure?"

"Yes, I'm sure. I want you there to hear what he has to say."

"Do you suppose they have found her and Ray?"

"Either that or they have a clue about where they went."

A few minutes later David ushered the sheriff into the formal living room. He gave Martie a double take, but David introduced her as Marnie's twin sister who was there helping care for Jonathan in Marnie's absence. He didn't go into her kidnapping and amnesia. That could come out later, if it was necessary.

"My gosh! I didn't know Mrs. Barrett had a twin. You been here all along?" Sheriff Clark asked Martie.

"I've been here a little over a month," she answered. "I live in Phoenix."

"Well, sir," the portly sheriff started, "I surely do hate to be bringing bad news, but that's the way of it."

"Tell me, Sheriff," David said. "What is it?"

"With this spring weather we been having, the snow's been melting. A little higher up in the mountains a pilot saw some wreckage of a plane. That last snowfall had covered it over, and no one had reported a plane missing, so it just sat there until now. The sheriff's office up there sent in a team to see about it, and, well, sir, it's Mr. Boling's plane—the one he kept out at Higgins' Airfield. You know, the one you were asking about."

"Yes, Sheriff. Ray Boling stole something from the plant. I was and am looking for him."

"I remember you telling me that, yes sir, I do. Mr. Barrett, Mr. Boling was in the plane. He's dead, killed instantly, I reckon. And that thing you're looking for, I imagine it's there, along with a briefcase full of papers."

David tried to absorb what the sheriff was telling him.

"There's more, Mr. Barrett, and this is the hard part. Mrs. Barrett's body was there, too. Looks like she was killed at the same time as Mr. Boling. Likely they got caught in that last snowstorm and just flew into the side of the mountain.

"I'm so sorry to have to bring news like this, sir. It's never easy going through something like this.

"We'll get your property back to you as soon as the sheriff's office up there releases it back to us. We have the paperwork from when you reported it stolen, so it shouldn't be any trouble to get it."

David finally found his voice. "When will my wife's body be released, Sheriff Clark? I need to make plans for a service."

"Of course, sir, of course. I'll let you know as soon as I get word." He stood up and held his hat to his chest. "My condolences, Mr. Barrett and . . ." He looked at Martie.

"Kelley, Sheriff. My name is Martha Kelley," Martie said as she wiped her eyes with a tissue. Although she had only met her sister that one fateful time, the thoughts of her life and death touched her heart in an odd, regretful way.

THREE MONTHS LATER

"What about it, Sport? Think you'll like living in this house?"

"Sure, Daddy. I like my room, and I like the big backyard. Do you suppose I could have a dog now, since there's a fence?"

"I think that might be a possibility, but we have to get settled first."

"And the park is just down the street. Can we go there sometimes, Mommy? Can we?"

"I'm sure we can. Maybe we can even get some playground equipment to go in our own backyard so you can swing and slide anytime you want to."

"Oh boy! Maybe I can even find a friend to teeter-totter with me."

"You'll be starting school in a few months. I imagine there will be lots of kids from this neighborhood in your kindergarten class. You'll make lots of new friends," David said.

He and Martie held hands as they walked through their new home, talking about what kind of furniture to buy to fill the rooms.

"How is your mother taking all these changes?" Martie asked.

"As well as you could expect. She had to accept the fact that Marnie is dead when she went to the funeral. Even my mother can't deny reality like that. And when we married, she had to accept that I marry who I want to, not whom she chooses for me."

"Is she settled into her new place?"

"Yes, that was the easy part. Although she said she wanted to keep the big house, she had lived in only a small portion of it for years. It was too big for one person, and having three employees for one woman was ridiculous. She'll get by fine with Mary coming a couple of times a week to clean for her. The condo is as big as she needs, and her friends are calling on her more often now.

"I have a feeling she'll change when we give her a grandchild she knows for sure is hers," David said. They strolled down the hall, looking into the bedrooms, smiling at Jonathan in his new room, singing and playing with the stuffed dinosaur that went everywhere with him.

As they reached the bedroom next to Jonathan's, which was across the hall from the master suite, David put his hand on her belly and smiled. "Everything will be different in about six months."